MURDER AT GREYFRIAR'S KIRK

DI MCKENZIE BOOK 2

ANNA-MARIE MORGAN

For my readers, with love.

ALSO BY ANNA-MARIE MORGAN

The DI McKenzie Series (So far)

Murder on Arthur's Seat

Murder at Greyfriars Kirk

The DI Giles Series (21 books)

Book 1 - Death Master

Book 2 - You Will Die

Book 3 - Total Wipeout

Book 4 - Deep Cut

Book 5 - The Pusher

Book 6 - Gone

Book 7 - Bone Dancer

Book 8 - Blood Lost

Book 9 - Angel of Death

Book 10 - Death in the Air

Book 11 - Death in the Mist

Book 12 - Death under Hypnosis

Book 13 - Fatal Turn

Book 14 - The Edinburgh Murders

Book 15 - A Picture of Murder

Book 16 - The Wilderness Murders

Book 17 - The Bunker Murders

Book 18 - The Garthmyl Murders

Book 19 - The Signature

Book 20 - The Incendiary Murders

Book 21 - The Park Murders

1

THE GIRL IN THE KIRKYARD

"And so, the wee dog came here every day, lying on his master John Gray's grave. Every day for fourteen years, no matter the weather. The Lord Provost, William Chambers, fed him and kept his eye on the wee animal. The City Council paid the dog licence, so they wouldn't take Bobby away." Twenty-five-year-old Margaret McLean paused for effect, ceasing walking to pan her phone around the grounds. "But then there be the dark side of Greyfriars Kirkyard... There could be a quarter of a million bodies under this turf. Everything from plague victims to those executed or tortured to death. Every year, people complain of being attacked on the grounds. Wounds, including deep scratches, bruises, and bite marks, appear on their flesh. Some say MacKenzie's poltergeist continues to wreak a torturous havoc, but some of these attacks may have a more down-to-earth connection, perpetrated by a living, breathing human being."

Footsteps somewhere behind startled her. "Who's there?" The woman's rounded eyes peered about as she shone her torch here and there. "Hello?" She saw only cold grey headstones and damp grass in the light of her small torch. Nothing to worry about. Margaret returned to movie-making, stowing a mental note to edit and remove her frightened exclamations. Storytelling made her jumpy. She returned to the narrative. "Before it contained tombstones, this was a large piece of flat land behind Greyfriars Kirk. George 'Bloody' MacKenzie had covenanters imprisoned here. Men tortured by having their legs gradually squashed using planks of wood hammered inside spiked wooden shackles." Margaret shivered, the urge to leave the kirkyard growing ever stronger. Perhaps it was the cold seeping into her bones, or maybe it was the low mist curling around the gravestones. Hollywood paid good money to make effects like this. But her mist was free, and common as muck in the Scottish capital city this time of year. However, tonight, the vaporous swirls added to her unease. Perhaps she should finish the film later in the week. And bring a friend.

An owl hooted. The girl's steps quickened. Time to go.

She barely had time to register the glint of steel as a black-clad arm came from behind. A half-gasp was all she managed before her killer wielded the savage slice to her neck. Horror and disbelief followed, accompanied by an inability to scream. One stroke had silenced Margaret McLean, as the life ebbed from her in crimson gushes. The thump as her body hit the ground was the last sound from the woman as the murderer cowered over her briefly, then melted away.

MCKENZIE PRESSED HIS LIPS TOGETHER. Times like this, he badly needed a smoke, but would not give in to the urge. It was ten years since he had last done that. And he had made before. He slashed her execution-style. It would have taken only moments."

"The saving grace, eh? I'm glad she didn't suffer."

"If she did, it wouldn't have been for long."

"No-one reported hearing anything. It doesn't look like she screamed."

"He cut her vocal cords. Screaming was out of the question."

"Can you identify the weapon for us?"

"I don't think it was a big knife. The blade was around four or five inches at most. I'll do some measurements after I have examined her organs and we'll run tests on tissue samples from the neck, in case the blade left metal particles behind. I'll email you when I have more of an idea. We may need Luke's help," she said, referring to the forensic biologist.

"Aye, no worries. We've got plenty of other stuff to be getting on with while we're waiting."

The pathologist lifted her eyes to his. "This killer needs catching. Someone this practiced will probably do it again."

"God, I hope not." The DI grimaced. "Maybe he targeted her specifically? Could be a killer for hire?"

"Are you thinking that a disgruntled ex paid to have her whacked?"

"Dr Campbell..." Grant feigned shock. "What kind of expression is that for a respectable pathologist?" He laughed. "Have her whacked? We're not in Prohibition America, you know."

Fiona chuckled, looking the youngest he had seen her. "Even forensic pathologists watch TV sometimes."

"Aye well, you should be watching Miss Marple, not Goodfellas." He winked at her. "I'll be having words with your Martin at this rate," he said, referring to her husband, an Edinburgh University chemistry professor.

"Oh, don't... He already accuses me of watching trash." She pulled a face. The weariness was back. "Sometimes, after leaving here, it's all I am fit for."

"You and me, both." Grant checked his watch. "Listen, I'd better leave you to it. My team is scouring CCTV footage, and I said I'd be back to help. I don't want them accusing me of shirking."

"Sure, no problem. I think I've given you pretty much everything I can at this point, anyway. But take care out there... Whoever killed this lass is one dangerous SOB."

He nodded. "We'll go canny."

DC GRAHAM DALGLIESH leaned back in his chair, staring at the screen, his face lined in concentration.

"What have you got?" McKenzie stood over his shoulder.

"The victim was a true-crime buff. Had her own sleuthing channel. In the footage she recorded around the kirkyard, she pauses occasionally, as though listening. The camera swings round erratically during those times."

"What are you thinking?"

"It's like she heard something or someone, and turned to investigate. We don't see what she is looking at because she doesn't point the gimbal at whatever is there. It swings around a bit in her hand. But there's a discernible wobble to her voice when she goes back to filming. Then things settle down until the next time she reacts to whatever is bugging her."

The DI leaned in, watching the video as the victim's

camera panned around the kirkyard. "Can we hear anything besides Margaret in the footage?"

Dalgliesh shook his head. "I've listened with headphones and without, and I cannae detect anything above her voice until she's attacked later on. I'm fairly sure he came at her from behind. She drops the camera, and the screen goes black. But it carries on recording sound for another seventeen minutes."

"Do we have the only version of this footage?"

Graham shook his head. "No, this is a digital copy. Forensics have the original. They were going to enhance the audio for us."

"Good." McKenzie nodded.

"Maybe she sensed rather than heard the killer's presence? Women's intuition, you ken?"

"It's possible. There's another pause." Grant pointed at the screen. "I think you may be right, and she heard something. Her killer must have been following. It wouldn't be hard to do, dodging from tomb to tomb, or headstone to headstone, while she was looking the other way, making her movie."

"Aye... And we know she wasn't wearing headphones, because on two occasions during the footage, she turns the camera on herself to talk directly to her viewers."

"Perhaps she was expecting her attacker?"

"What makes you say that?"

McKenzie shrugged. "It's the feeling I get from watching this... It's like she was expecting something to happen."

"But not expecting to die, eh?"

"No, I doubt she expected that. But maybe she was drawing someone out. I don't mean that night. But, perhaps when she uploaded the footage, she expected it to influence someone other than the audience? Someone she was looking to bait?"

Dalgliesh pondered for a moment. "Aye, maybe... What say you, Sue? Do you agree she was baiting someone? Maybe the serial sex attacker she believed was on the loose?"

Robertson shook her head. "I don't know. We'll have more of an idea once we've spoken to those closest to Margaret and had a good look around her flat. If she was investigating someone, there may be notes or diaries; something that names him." She looked at McKenzie. "We've got appointments with the family tomorrow, right?"

"We have. We'll be flat out. So get a good night's sleep. I want us on the ball tomorrow. The sooner we get this sicko off of our streets, the better."

"There's a rustling near the camera that goes on for over two minutes after the victim falls to the ground." Dalgliesh pushed his chair back from the table. "Sounds like someone rummaging around in her clothing."

"Checking her pockets? There was no evidence of sexual interference."

"Have a listen... See what you think?"

McKenzie listened through Dalgliesh's headphones. "Aye, I see what you mean. I think he's looking for something; maybe worried about what she might have on him?"

"That's what I was thinking. Maybe he killed Margaret to shut her up?"

3

GREYFRIARS

The entrance to Greyfriars Kirkyard was through a tiny close between Greyfriars Art Shop and a pub called the Greyfriars Bobby. Both establishments contributed to the character of the historic Edinburgh neighbourhood, making them distinctive landmarks for locals and visitors alike.

The art shop blended well with its surroundings. The Victorian-era frontage, painted in a deep viridian, included large display windows on either side of the door, and the shop's name and number in gold lettering.

Greyfriars Bobby Pub, on the opposite side of the Kirkyard entrance, had a more rustic, cosy frontage in black and white. The stone exterior had a welcoming Scottish vibe, and a classic pub sign swinging above the door. A string of orange lights adorned the windows, creating an inviting ambience for those seeking a pint and a natter.

McKenzie headed between the two, and through the intricately patterned wrought-iron gate of the kirkyard, into the realm of a bygone era, where centuries-old tombstones and mausoleums surrounded him. In the pale morning mist, it was both serene and haunting.

The DI was here to speak with a member of the Greyfriars management team. But, before he did, he wanted to view once more the tombstone where the killer of Margaret McLean placed her following the brutal slaughter. Crime scene and search staff had only recently vacated the area; their tape still fluttered around the perimeter.

He turned his attention to the where they had found the girl.

The tombstone of Thomas Bannatyne, dating back to sixteen-thirty-eight, was attached to the Flodden Wall. A carved angel holding up a book and crushing a skeleton below its foot symbolised the deceased soul's victory over death. Two Corinthian-style pillars flanked the angel on either side, and the whole possessed a variegated patina of industrial-age grime, giving it a darkly mysterious edge.

Grant buttoned his long black overcoat, telling himself it was the damp mist making him shiver, not the memory of Margaret's body seated under the unsettling Gothic edifice.

"Sorry, I saw you enter past the kirk... It's DI McKenzie, isn't it?"

Grant spun round to see a lean gentleman in his early fifties, with short greying hair, a small goatee beard, and rimless glasses, holding out a hand towards him. His attire included a white shirt, beige chinos, and a grey anorak, giving a smart yet casual appearance.

The DI swallowed. "Tim Shaw?" He asked, surprised at the other man's unexpected appearance.

"Aye, that's right. I'm the one you spoke to on the phone yesterday. I'm due to induct one of the new volunteers into the kirk this morning, but I am free for the next half-hour. We have several volunteers helping with a range of jobs. I honestly don't know what we would do without them." There was a nasal quality to his voice.

"Right..." McKenzie pushed his hands deep into his overcoat pockets. "I'm glad you could make the time to see me. You'll know that we found a young woman here yesterday?"

"Aye, young Margaret McLean..."

"You knew her?"

Shaw nodded. "We know her family, and Margaret used to help us here as a teen. We hadn't seen her much in recent years, but we are all devastated by the news. She was a lovely girl." He grimaced. "It was a horrible way for her to die... Do you know who did it? The staff are all nervous since we heard the news. We wonder who might lurk around the corner when we come through here now."

"Did you know Margaret was recording a video that night for her followers on social media?"

Shaw shook his head. "Was she? She never told us or anything."

"Aye, she was filming around the cemetery."

"Oh... Do you think someone followed her?"

A crow cawed as it hopped around the graves, looking for worms.

McKenzie watched it for a moment. "We cannot say. I thought, perhaps, you might have heard something? We have CCTV footage of her approaching the entrance to the kirkyard, and we have the video she was making during her last hour alive. But I was hoping you or your team could tell us if anyone else was here at the kirk around eight o'clock on Monday night, and if anyone was working or visiting here?"

"Greyfriars is only open until three in the afternoon. We have staff and volunteers who are here until later, and we have regular evening events. But there was nothing on that night. There would have been no-one here. We gave uniformed police officers details of everyone that was here during the day, and approximate times they left."

"Do you have a visitor's book?"

"We do."

"We'd like copies of the week's visitor pages, if we could?"

"Of course."

"What about yourself? Were you working that day?"

"I was... I left around half-five. It may have been ten or fifteen minutes later, but it was within that ballpark." Shaw rubbed his hands together. "It's another cold one today." He blew on them. "We could go inside?"

"I was about to ask if I could look around the kirk?"

"Be our guest..." Shaw turned to walk with the DI towards the buttressed building. "By the way, we have a memorial service for Miss McLean next Thursday. You're welcome to pop by. Her family and friends, and any staff who knew her, will be there."

"I might do that." Grant nodded.

THE INTERIOR of the buttressed Greyfriars Kirk was an impressive Gothic space of high vaulted ceilings, pointed arches, and intricate stone carvings. The architectural detail reflected the church's long history, dating back to its construction in the seventeenth century.

Evocative stained glass windows depicted historical scenes; their filtered light filling the interior, adding to the spiritual feel.

Rows of blue-cushioned wooden chairs, in traditional

previous concert, and the last thing he wanted was to let him down again. He pressed his lips together.

"You are coming, aren't you?"

"Aye, I want to be there..."

"You sound doubtful." Her forehead creased.

"We are going to see the flat of the murdered girl we found at Greyfriars tomorrow and talk to her partner. I'm hoping we can get that done in time."

"If you're not there, he'll be devastated," she said, turning her face to the screen and pulling back from him with stiff shoulders.

"I know... I'll do everything I can to make sure I'm there at two o'clock."

His wife didn't answer, her eyes remaining on the screen.

"I know you don't enjoy going on your own. I really want to be there, but do you think you should ask your mum, in case?"

Jane didn't answer.

"I won't let either of you down." He hated it when there was tension between them. "I'll keep my ticket with me, in case I'm late. But I will be at the concert."

"Thank you." The shoulders relaxed, but her eyes remained on the screen.

Grant thought it best to say no more. He would show her he meant what he said.

4

NEAREST AND DEAREST

Margaret McLean had occupied a one-bedroom flat in Corstophine, overlooking Corstophine Hill, three doors down from her parents' two-storey home.

McKenzie and Robertson took the peripheral route, avoiding the city centre and heading southwest on Leith Walk, past Edinburgh Playhouse and the St. James Shopping Centre. As they turned left onto Princes Street, the majestic Edinburgh Castle came into view above before they turned west, passing the Scott Monument and the Princes Street Gardens. Lothian Road took them past the Usher Hall and the Traverse Theatre, and onto Queensferry Road, where they crossed over the Dean Bridge with views of the Water of Leith.

They decided it was best to visit her grieving mother and father first, on their way to Margaret's apartment, as information from them might be pertinent to anything they found at the dead influencer's home.

The DI straightened his tie and cleared his throat as

they waited for the couple, in their late fifties, to answer the door.

Susan cast her eyes up and down the street. Aside from the odd car passing, there was no-one about. It was nine-thirty in the morning, and most of the residents would be at work, school, or indoors catching up with breakfast news.

Fifty-nine-year-old David McLean opened the door. White-haired, and wearing beige cords and cardigan over a white shirt, he held the door open for the detectives to enter a hall tiled in a black-and-white diamond pattern. "Please, go on through to the sitting room," he said, pointing to a door on their left. "My wife, Pam, is in there."

They did as he asked, giving their condolences to fifty-eight-year-old Pamela McLean as she sat hunched in jeans and dark-green fleece in a high-backed armchair, her eyes puffed and sore. Her red hair, reminiscent of her daughter's, contained small swathes of grey.

David pushed the cushions back on the sofa for them to take a seat. The room had a distinct chill, the hearth offering only ashes in the cast-iron grate. A clock ticked perceptibly on the mantlepiece.

Mr McLean ran a hand through his hair, sighing. "You'll have to forgive us." His gaze crossed to the window and the street outside. "We're still coming to terms with what happened."

"We understand..." Susan pressed her lips together, her head tilted in empathy. "Take all the time you need. We're here to learn more about your daughter... Who she was, her interests, and who her friends were."

"We understand Margaret had her own YouTube channel?" Grant leaned forward in his seat, his gaze on Pamela.

Mrs McLean's glazed gaze turned towards him, but her mouth remained closed, as though opening it would require more energy than she possessed and she would rather relive her memories than join the discourse. She blinked sore eyes and merely nodded.

"Mags was fascinated by true crime. I guess you would call her an internet sleuth." David McLean stretched his legs out in front of the armchair, the fingers of his hands entwined on his thighs. "Since she was little, she could never ignore injustice of any kind. From the earliest age, if she saw kids being mean to other kids, she would intervene to stop it. It got her in a few scuffles before the age of ten, I can tell you. She was just that sort of girl. She didn't get into fights as an adult, but she always had a keen sense of right and wrong. You would think she was a confident wee lassie from all that, but she wasn't as self-assured as you might think. She was still only twenty-five, had bouts of anxiety, and doubts and regrets about things she had said or done. Margaret would always turn to those closest to her for reassurance. I'm surprised she went to the Kirkyard alone after dark. If she went alone, that is..."

McKenzie narrowed his eyes. "Do you think she might have had someone else with her?"

"I don't know... Maybe. For all her strength in challenging wrong-doing, she was more than a little scared of the dark. If she was there in the Kirkyard alone, there must have been a pressing reason. Something she couldn't let go of."

"There was no evidence on her video of anyone accompanying her."

"Aye well, there wouldn't be, necessarily. When her boyfriend, Andy, went with her, he knew not to talk while she was filming." David McLean broke out in a wistful smile. "It was more than his life was worth. She spent hours planning her videos, choreographing them on paper, and writing and re-writing the narratives. And she'd become very good at it. The recent ones we saw were really quite professional. She had a knack for it, so she did."

"Sounds like, when she got the bit between her teeth, there was no stopping her?" The DI made a few notes.

"Aye, she was highly committed."

"Had she been to the kirkyard before?"

"She had been many times fascinated by all the attacks said to have happened there. Thousands of them, she said."

"Margaret believed in them?"

"Not all of them... Look, Mags was no fool. She knew many of the incidents were pranks, or maybe even psychosomatic, but she said some of them appeared more sinister, and she talked about them fitting a pattern."

"And it was those she was investigating?"

"Aye, she didn't think they were down to George Bloody MacKenzie's poltergeist, like many people believe. I mean, that's the myth, isn't it? It's what a lot of folk talk about. She said there were patterns to the dates, and types of attack, in some cases. Her YouTube channel was growing, and she had a sizeable following. I guess you'd call her an influencer these days, eh?"

"Aye..." McKenzie smoothed his beard.

"And the Greyfriars attacks were not the only things she was interested in. She was quite the amateur detective."

"So, the stories she was telling in the graveyard, were they for the attacker's benefit that night? Could she have been trying to draw him out?"

David cast sad eyes to the floor. "I think they might have been... Her channel was for true crime fans. It wasn't a history channel, as such, though she was interested in cold cases."

The DI gave a wry smile. "Sounds like she'd have made a great addition to my team at MIT."

Mr McLean nodded. "Aye, I think she'd have done you proud."

"Did she never consider joining the police?"

"She did, but she also wanted to be a mother, and thought shift work would play havoc with her relationships. If you'd asked her at age twelve, she'd have bitten your hand off but, nowadays, not so much." He sighed. "And now... all those opportunities are gone."

"We're so sorry..." DS Robertson's voice was soft.

"Aye, I can only imagine what you are both going through." McKenzie's eyes travelled from David to Pam.

The mother's remained downward as she wiped tears from both cheeks. "It's not the same without her. She always popped by every other day. She never missed. Even if it was only for a few minutes, she never failed to visit. And I would go over to her for coffee." Mrs McLean lifted her eyes to his. "Please find whoever murdered Mags. Don't let them get away with taking my daughter's life away."

He nodded. "We'll throw everything we have at this. We want this killer off the streets, and justice for your Margaret. And my team and I will do whatever it takes to get the job done."

"Thank you," she whispered, her gaze returning to the thread worn carpet; rubbing her hands as though to bring back circulation.

"Would you like me to light you a fire?" The DI nodded towards the hearth.

"I'll do it." David McLean approached the fireplace. "I meant to get it going earlier, but one of our neighbours popped by before you. My wife suffers with arthritis, and we never usually leave it this late to have one going. But thank you, anyway."

Grant nodded. "We'll see ourselves out."

MARGARET'S SECOND-FLOOR flat overlooked the green spaces of Corstophine Hill. Her parents had given McKenzie their spare key, as forensic personnel still had possession of the victim's own. The detectives let themselves in and donned latex gloves.

Grant had expected the place to be clean and tidy, but what he found was more than that. The young woman's flat could not have been more striking if an interior designer had furnished it. Not that she had purchased expensive items or branded goods. It was obvious some of her things had come from second-hand or antique stores, but she had obviously possessed a keen eye for detail and knew how items worked together. The pieces offset each other well. Patterned vases helped highlight canvas paintings, while height and colour arranged books complimented art works. The colours in the rug and sofa worked to unify the lounge, as did the bedspread in the bedroom. The rooms seemed to have leapt from the pages of a design magazine.

A small office upstairs held a workstation that included Margaret's laptop. She had arranged the feature wall as the backdrop for videos she made in the room. Along with books and plant pots on shelving, was a silver YouTube plaque to celebrate her achievements and the number of subscribers to her channel. A retro tungsten-style lamp provided another focal point in the corner, and light from the window above her desk bathed the room.

McKenzie made a mental note to check out her channel to learn more about her personality and what she had been working on.

Forensics personnel had taken her memory sticks, but they would soon share relevant content with the team. Meanwhile, Grant flicked through files of printed notes Margaret had made about her investigations. They comprised two A4 Box files, and an A4 folder. The latter appeared to contain the most recent cases she was working, including one she had titled, 'Greyfriars attacks'.

"Found anything?" Robertson was at his side.

"She was a busy girl." Grant pulled a face. "And a copious note maker. It'll take a while to go through all this."

Susan grinned. "Don't knock it. It would be worse if we had nothing to go on."

The DI checked his watch.

"Somewhere to be?" She raised her brows.

"Aye, I mustn't forget my son's concert this afternoon. I may have to take this home with me." He lifted the smaller folder. "There are details in here of her investigations into the kirkyard poltergeist. Except, a quick flick through suggests she suspected a flesh and blood perpetrator. Some of her notes are scripts for social media videos. But if I am not mistaken, she was also looking into the potential murder of another YouTuber."

"Was she?" Robertson frowned. "Let me see?"

"Last year, someone killed a man named Tam Fleming."

"Tam Fleming? It wasn't one of our cases, was it? Where was he from?"

"Edinburgh."

"How come we didn't hear about it?"

"Says here, they believed muggers stabbed him when he resisted a theft. They put two men inside for it, caught the same night. Margaret thought they had the wrong people, and that they should have investigated his death as a targeted murder. He was only thirty-one. I'm going to take the file home and have a look through. And I'll watch a few of her videos on YouTube."

"Let me know if you need help," Susan offered. "I'm sure we could do some of the stuff in the office?"

"Aye, but I thought I would look into the death of this other YouTuber in my spare time. It may be unrelated to Margaret's death but, if she was right, and Fleming's killer noticed her interest in the case, we have another potential motive for murder aside from her Greyfriars investigations."

"We can look into the Greyfriars incidents in the office."

"Great... Well, we have a lot to do. With any luck, Scenes of Crime will have fibres and prints for us... though I am not holding my breath. I think this killer planned Margaret's murder down to the letter."

The sound of keys rattling against the lock of the front door had them looking at each other.

McKenzie headed for the stairs. "Can I help you?" he asked, as a strapping, muscular, twenty-something male strode into the hallway.

The man started, taking a step back. "Who are you?"

"Och, I was about to ask you the same question. I am DI Grant McKenzie, and behind me is DS Susan Robertson. We're investigating the murder of Margaret McLean."

"Oh..." He ran a hand through short, blonde hair. "I'm Andy. Andy Scott. I was Mags's boyfriend. I came to pick up a few things, and to spend some time thinking about her."

Grant noted the lad was clean shaven, and tidily dressed. Aside from the faint shadows under his eyes, he looked to be in good shape emotionally. He certainly didn't appear to have spent the night crying for his girl.

They moved back up the stairs and into the lounge at the front of the apartment. "Her boyfriend, you say?"

"Yes... her partner, actually." Andy grimaced. "We didn't live together. It wasn't for want of trying, but Mags thought it best we had our own space. She was always busy, and didn't think it was fair to keep me hanging around waiting for her. I regret not pushing more on the cohabiting front, but I didn't think our time would be this short. I kind of thought we'd have at least a couple of decades together, you know? But her killer had other plans." His pale blue eyes wandered to the window. "Poor Mags... I should have been there."

"Why weren't you?" McKenzie studied Scott's profile as the lad stared out of the window.

"I offered, but she declined. When she said no, it didn't surprise me. Mags had an independent streak, but she suffered from situational anxiety. We never really understood what brought it on. Sometimes she would be fine in a packed room, and other times she wouldn't. She would have this hot, prickly feeling come over her, and we'd have to leave. But then she found her tribe on the net in a way she wasn't able to in real life. She was a bit of a loner, really. I felt sure that walking through a graveyard after dark would have her quaking at the knees. But she didn't want me there. I called her later that night to see how she got on. But, obviously, she didn't answer. Her phone went to voicemail, so I left her a message saying I hoped she was okay. She didn't get the chance to call me back."

"What time was that? What time did you call her?"

"Would have been about nine, I think? Hang on..." He reached into his pocket; pulling out his phone and flicking through the call log. "Eleven minutes past nine," he said.

"Did you try again?"

Andy shook his head. "I didn't. I assumed she would get my message and ring me back."

"What did you think when she didn't call? Were you worried about her?"

He shrugged. "I wasn't overly worried, no. I mean, it wouldn't have been the first time she had waited until the morning to get back to me. Making videos wore her out. As her channel was growing, I suggested she get someone to help her. I even offered to do things for free, but she wasn't at that stage in her head. I think she thought someone else would alter or hamper her artistic vision."

"How old are you, Andy?"

"Twenty-eight."

"From Glasgow?"

"Aye, originally from Glasgow, but I live here in Corstophine now. Though I'm a couple of streets away."

"I'd like your details, if I could? Phone and house number." The DI handed his pocketbook and a pen over. "Write them in there, if you would?"

Scott followed the instructions, but his face turned red. "Do you want my date of birth?"

"Aye, you can jot it down as well. That would be helpful. We may request your phone records from your mobile provider."

"Okay." He had his head bowed as he wrote his details. They couldn't see his eyes.

Grant and Susan exchanged glances. "Have you got someone to support you?" Susan asked Andy.

"I have my parents in Leith, and my mates in Corstophine, if I need them. To be honest, though, I'd rather be on my own just now. I would rather remember Margaret in my way."

"How long have you had a key to her flat?"

"A year, maybe longer... But no more than eighteen months."

"Can you not remember when she gave you it?" Grant asked.

"She gave me a key, the first time, probably eighteen months ago. It was in the autumn sometime. But she took it back after we had a major row before the following Christmas. She gave it back to me two months later. I've had it twelve months since then."

"I see." McKenzie pushed his hands in his trouser pockets. "Did you have many arguments?"

"Not really... We agreed on most things, actually."

"Did you stay here sometimes?"

"Aye, I stayed here regularly. Mags preferred us here because her place was larger and tidier than mine. She didn't appreciate my mess."

"How were you getting on in the weeks before she was killed?"

"Fine. We were both doing our own thing, but staying together regularly. She was busier than I was. I missed her. But we were getting along great."

The DI was uncomfortable with how calm Andy was. People react differently to grief, and perhaps he only let go when there was no-one else around. But McKenzie's gut told him something was off. Something told him the boyfriend knew more than he was letting on.

Robertson gave Grant a gentle nudge. "It's one-forty," she said, looking at her watch.

"Oh, Christ!" McKenzie grimaced at Scott. "We have to go, but we will talk to you again."

"Sure, no problem." Andy shrugged. "I'll see you out."

5

TIME LOST

McKenzie ran as fast as he could from the car park to the school's front entrance. They had locked the door. He could see a staff member through the window, but she had her back to him. The DI was seven minutes late and, with a damp forehead, dry mouth, and clenched stomach. He tapped gently on the window.

It took several attempts to get the teacher's attention. She looked at her watch and, for a moment, he feared she wouldn't allow him in. But his saviour approached and unlocked the door, before checking his credentials and directing him to the hall.

He paused in the entrance, eyes scouring the backs of everyone's head until he saw Jane's, two rows from the front. He made his way towards her, waving apologies to those he brushed past for interrupting their view.

Jane had reserved his seat with her coat and bag. He sat down, feeling guilt as parents who had been there longer than himself were standing at the back. "Sorry I'm late," he whispered in his wife's ear as he settled in. "I hope I haven't missed him."

She shook her head, handing over a schedule. "Davie is number five in the line-up."

"Oh, thank God." He gave an involuntary sigh as the tension eased from him. "I was worried I wouldn't get here in time."

She squeezed his hand, letting him know he did okay.

Aside from clapping at the various acts, they watched in silence until it was their son's turn.

Jane gave Davie a wave when she saw him nervously searching the faces of the crowd. Grant stood briefly, so their son would catch sight of them.

The boy broke out in a nervous grin, giving them a wave back.

He looked so small up there on his own. The DI thought he caught his son's knees knocking. After a tentative beginning, and a stiff elbow causing a scratchy start, Davie was soon in his stride and playing the Bach excerpt with a smooth confidence that belied his age.

McKenzie's chest puffed with pride. That was his son up there.

When the concert finished at half-past three, Grant apologised to his family as he headed back to work. "We'll go for pizza tomorrow night... Would you like that?" he asked the children. Without exception, they were happy about the prospect of going out for pizza, except Martha wanted it now.

Jane was quiet.

Her husband grimaced. "I'm sorry, there are still I have things to do today for the murder enquiry. But I'll not to be too late. I should be home by seven at the latest."

"That's fine." She sighed. "I was hoping you would take

the rest of the afternoon. You've been working such long hours."

"I know..." He pushed the hair back from her eyes. "It won't be forever. When this case is solved-"

"There will be another one." She finished for him. "It's okay, Grant McKenzie. I love you. Be safe. And don't make promises you can't keep."

He nodded. "Thank you."

His heart was heavy as he left them to make their way home without him. He glanced around at the other dads present, suspecting the majority had taken the rest of the afternoon off to go home with the family. He envied them. His sadness at lost time more keen than ever.

FIVE O'CLOCK, and the DI was back at the Kirkyard; notepad in hand. He made his way to Thomas Bannatyne's tombstone where Margaret McLean's killer had left her, casting his eyes around the gravestones, and looking for where the murderer may have hidden before setting upon her. There were several places, but none he could definitively say was the one the attacker sprang from.

The cleaned and enhanced audio from the victim's phone gave no clue as to the direction from which her killer swooped. It was clear from the video he had come from behind, but his approach path was unknown, and there were no discernible footsteps in the audio. He may have worn soft-soled shoes, or only walked on the grass. Officers who searched the kirkyard found no cigarette butts, food wrappers, or footprints in the vicinity. The ground had been hard on the night she died. The temperature had barely lifted above freezing all day. Dalgliesh and McAllister had scrutinised the cars in nearby carparks on CCTV and located the drivers. All had a reason for being there, which checked out. The killer had either parked further away, perhaps walking some distance before arriving in the kirk-yard, or was amongst those with a legitimate reason for being around. McKenzie had left Graham and Helen going through the various statements gathered by uniform, looking for anyone connected to the victim.

Grant walked back to the entrance and took a left, heading for Greyfriars Bobby, the nearby pub, and went inside.

A mix of antique wooden panels and vintage photographs of the pub's rich history adorned the walls. The main bar featured a well-polished mahogany counter, and the shelves behind were lined with an extensive selec-tion of whiskies showcasing the pub's commitment to Scot-land's famed spirit. A comforting scent of wood smoke filled the air, along with the occasional whiff of hearty pub fare cooking in the kitchen. The fireplace cast an orange glow over those it warmed as they relaxed with friends.

A few of the punters present sat on plush leather chairs, at sturdy wooden tables, while others preferred barstools, and a blether with the bartender. The murmur of conversa-tion mingled with soft background music. It made the DI wish he was here for a quiet evening drink with his wife. But he had work to do.

He chose a quiet moment to approach the barman, a guy he had spoken to before during other investigations, and who he considered a friend. There wasn't much that went on around Greyfriars that Gordon Caldwell didn't hear about. The forty-two-year-old had his sleeves rolled up, and a pen behind his ear. He ran a hand over stylish short-cut hair, puffing out his cheeks as he finished stacking glasses below the bar.

McKenzie cleared his throat. "Gordon." He nodded in greeting.

"Hey, McKenzie, how's things?" Caldwell grinned at him. "Can I get you a drink?"

"I'll have a coke."

"Half?"

"Aye, thanks."

Caldwell grabbed a glass and began pulling at the pump. "You'll be busy right now, eh?" he asked, waiting for bubbles to settle before finishing the pour and setting the glass down in front of the DI.

Grant noticed bags below Gordon's eyes. He mused they must be short-staffed. "Aye, you could say that. You'll know we've been up at the kirkyard?"

"I heard..." The barman grimaced. "It was a horrible business, wasn't it? I couldnae believe it. We've had crazy goings-on at the kirk in the past, but nothing like that. There's been almost nothing else on the news. What was she doing making a movie there after dark? She wasnae very old, was she?"

"No... She wasn't." McKenzie pressed his lips together. "I was hoping you noticed something the evening of her murder?"

"Like what?" Gordon leaned forward, elbows on the bar; his demeanour conspiratorial. "What do you want to know?"

Grant couldn't help a chuckle. "You old gossip-monger."

"Who, me?" Caldwell feigned surprise. "Okay, you got me. I admit it, I'm nosey."

"Good." The DI seated himself on a barstool. "Margaret

McLean... Did she come in here on the night she was killed?"

"Aye, as it happens, she did, apparently."

"Apparently? You mean you didn't see her yourself?"

"No, I didn't. Unfortunately, it wasn't my shift that night. Pete Ramsey was in."

"Is he new?"

"He's been here a few months. Works three nights a week, usually. Sometimes earlier in the day if we need it."

"What did he tell you?"

"Just that she'd popped in and had a half of lager. He said it was early... Would have been about seven-ish."

"Did she speak to anyone? Was anybody with her?"

"You might want to speak to Pete, but if my memory serves me, from what he said, she was on her own. But I think Hamish over there spoke to her briefly." He pointed to a grey-haired, older male sat at the bar with another man. "I think he made polite conversation with her, as he felt sorry she was on her own. He may know more?"

"Thanks." Grant left the barstool and approached the older man. "I'm sorry to disturb you." He held up his badge. "DI McKenzie, Scottish police. Can I ask you a couple of questions?"

"You investigating the murder?" Hamish asked.

"I am."

"I spoke to her, you ken, before what happened. Lovely woman... Didn't deserve to be murdered."

The DI tried not to stare at the copious nasal hair protruding from both nostrils. It was entirely in keeping with the hair on Hamish's head. A good trim was around three months overdue. "What kind of mood was she in? Did she appear relaxed? Nervous? Worried?"

"I'd say she seemed relaxed, but busy."

"Busy?"

"Aye, she was reading and scribbling stuff. She was really concentrating. I thought she might be a student at the university, but she looked older than most of them."

"What was she scribbling on? Was it a notebook? Or loose paper?"

"I'd say it was a book. I think it was a notebook, yes."

"There wasn't a book or notebook with her when they found her. Did she leave it here at the pub?"

The older man shook his head, scratching the stubble on his chin. "She took it with her. She had a large shoulder bag. I think she put the book inside it."

"Sorry, can I have your full name?"

"Hamish. Hamish MacFarlane."

McKenzie made notes. "I understand you spoke to her?"

"Aye, I felt sorry for her. It's rare we see a young lass like that in here on her own. I thought I would make conversation in case she felt out of place, and to be friendly, like."

"What did she say?"

"Och, she was polite, but I could tell she wasn't up for conversation. She was engrossed, and I got the feeling she didn't want to be disturbed. I got the impression she had a lot to do."

"Was she checking her watch? Or the door?"

Hamish frowned. "I can't say she was, but I wasn't watching after we finished speaking."

"Did she look like she was waiting for someone? I mean, while you were talking to her?"

"I didn't get that impression, but I was only chatting for a couple of minutes, and I'd had a few pints by then. I'd been here since half-four, and this would be around seven."

"What did she say to you?"

"I asked her if it was still cold outside, and she said it

was. I then said I hadn't known it so cold for a while, and she said it made her fingers numb, which was why she had popped in for a drink and to get warm. She looked like she had been out in the cold. Her nose was red, and she was wiping it with a hanky, like it was dripping. You... You don't think I was the last person to speak to her, do you?"

"We don't know, but you may have been. Would you be willing to give us a statement?"

"Aye, of course."

"Good. If you could write your address and phone number in here, I would be grateful. An officer will contact you for a formal statement."

Grant gave Caldwell a wave as he left the Greyfriars Bobby.

McKenzie fished the memory stick containing digital copies of Margaret McLean's files out of his overcoat pocket, taking it to the study at the back of the house. He had left his wife Jane binge-watching one of her favourite shows, kissing her on the cheek as he apologised for having to work at home again.

She had smiled and nodded, but it was clear her mind was already on the TV drama.

Grant grinned. Married life, eh? He couldn't complain. He was grateful she gave him space. Not for the first time, the DI considered how lucky he was. Jane was one in a million.

He plugged the stick into his laptop and opened the

folder, looking for the files detailing McLean's investigation into the kirkyard attacks.

He began with two videos in which she described the alleged assaults at the cemetery, detailing the number and nature of incidents reported to police. He could have taken the footage from her social media channels, but preferred to see the raw, unedited films. That way, he wouldn't miss anything. Sounds, or persons, edited out of the final videos, might provide crucial clues regarding the killer. They couldn't afford to lose anything if they were to solve her murder.

It felt strangely emotive, watching the girl he had only previously known as a lifeless, brutalised corpse propped against a tombstone. When she turned the camera on herself, he witnessed the vibrant, red-haired Margaret in full flow. Her energy and enthusiasm for her subject lit her face, and hooked him, as the observer, effortlessly into her story-telling. It was easy to like her, and get carried away by the tales she wove with mind-tingling intrigue.

Margaret focused on the attacks she believed had substance and that she could link, as she believed others were exaggerated or even made up.

Grant made copious notes as McLean detailed seven attacks in particular, which had occurred over the previous eighteen months. They differed from the rest. Most other incidents appeared to have involved a swift scratch on the back or neck, or a bite on the arm. She had included pictures of bruises and other, mainly minor, wounds associated with those reports. But the seven which stood out to her involved females being grabbed from behind, and dragged some distance before being groped, and having items of clothing taken from them. The perpetrator had stopped short of rape, but appeared to be escalating; he having attempted to kiss and fondle a recent victim. Although the myriad other attacks involved both male and female targets, the victims studied most intensely by McLean were all female. She was disappointed that, although police carried out initial investigations, they shelved the cases because of lack of corroboration, or evidence from CCTV, though they had kept fibres, and possible DNA samples in case. If the attacker existed, he appeared to be more phantom than human.

McKenzie paused the video as Margaret turned the camera on herself, her image frozen on the screen; mouth half-open, about to begin the next sentence. There was energy and light in her vivid blue eyes. Her killer had extinguished both.

Grant pondered the young woman going alone to the kirkyard, if indeed she had. Margaret had already outlined the assaults in previous videos. So what was her intention that night? And why? What had prevented her from taking a friend? Was she not worried about being assaulted while there alone? Or was she attempting to draw out the attacker with a sting, of sorts? If the latter, she had to have known how risky this would be, albeit she could not have expected to be murdered based on her target's previous MO. But why hadn't she taken her boyfriend, Andy?

He flicked through her folder of notes, most of them handwritten. The name Tam Fleming caught his eye. It rang a bell. He sat back, eyes scanning lines which summarised Margaret's investigation into his murder.

The courts had sentenced two men the previous year for killing Tam while he was out on a night out with friends. The group had gone to a bar in the city centre, and split up to wander home. Fleming was ambushed at a bus stop near Greyfriars Bobby, where he would have caught the ride home to Dean Village. The investigation had not come the DI's way, because uniformed officers had arrested two men that same night. CCTV had caught the offenders mugging several people at knifepoint. Police believed the same perpetrators killed Tam because he fought back. Despite their vehement protestations of innocence, the court convicted the men, though investigators never found the knife that killed Fleming.

Margaret had made it clear she believed both men were wrongly convicted and that Tam Fleming's killing had nothing to do with what he owned, but what he knew. Fleming had been a fellow true crime investigator with a popular social media channel. She believed his murder directly resulted from the things he had found out regarding the Greyfriars assaults.

Grant made a note to look into Fleming's channel. Had he been working along similar lines to McLean?

McKenzie checked his watch. He had been reading and watching the young woman's work for two and a half hours. There was still a pile of material to dig through, but it would have to wait. It was time to extract Jane from her binge-watching in the lounge and head to bed.

6

DEATH IN THE SNOW

McKenzie was early into the office in Leith Station the following day.

Dalgliesh was only ten minutes behind. He raised his brows, surprised to see the DI so early. "What time were you up?" He grinned.

Grant eyed him over the rim of his workstation. "I wanted to flick through the forensics report for Margaret McLean. I was hoping they would lift a fingerprint or two from her bag."

"You think the killer rifled through it?"

"I think he must have done. Someone took a book from her. A notebook she had been writing in." McKenzie sighed. "But it looks like SOCO only found the victim's prints on her belongings."

"I guess it's not all that surprising... The killer would have worn gloves."

"There were traces of blood on her belongings, which proved to be hers and, yes, the killer must have worn gloves." McKenzie got up to walk over and perch on the end of Dalgliesh's desk. "The blood was likely transferred when the perp took her notebook."

"There must have been something in there he wanted..." Dalgliesh put his jacket over the back of his chair.

"Or he was worried about what she had written... That she had named him in connection with attacks at the kirkyard, for instance."

"She was investigating assaults at the kirk?"

"Aye... those and the murder of Tam Fleming."

"Fleming? Wasn't he the guy knifed in the city centre last year? Robbery, wasn't it?"

"Margaret McLean didn't think so. Did you know he was also a true-crime YouTuber?"

"I heard about that, yeah. But his murder was something else, wasn't it? Or are you thinking his killer was still loose and murdered McLean? There are two pals serving time for his death. They caught them touting his watch and using his chip-and-pin at the local supermarket, and witnesses saw them leaving the close where Fleming was murdered."

McKenzie's brow furrowed. "Aye, and they had tried to mug others at knifepoint. I can see why the courts convicted them, and perhaps they are guilty of his death. Perhaps his end had nothing to do with McLean's. But, equally, they could have simply been a couple of chancers who happened upon his body and helped themselves from his pockets. I am going to watch Fleming's videos and find out what he was looking into. It is possible that someone killed Tam and Margaret for the same reasons."

"Aye well, let me know if you need my help after I've finished going through CCTV. That should be later today. I've still not found anyone that could be her killer. I don't understand it. It's like the killer materialised in the kirkyard.

Maybe it's true what they say about George 'Bloody' MacKenzie?"

The DI tossed his head. "Well, if it is, he'd better start behaving himself or he'll have Bloody Grant McKenzie to deal with, eh?"

Graham laughed. "If I were him, I'd be legging it out of Greyfriars as we speak."

~

THOUGH MARCH HAD USHERED in milder temperatures, Monday morning began with a blizzard, and a sudden cold snap. Slow-moving traffic filled the roads of Edinburgh along with lines of salt-ridden, slushy snow. Several inches of white had cushioned everything else.

As beautiful as it was, Grant was impatient to get on with things. He had received a call during breakfast from DS Susan Robertson informing him about another murder whose circumstances resembled those of Margaret McLean's killing.

James McDonald, better known by the sobriquet, 'Captain Crime', his social media persona, had his throat slashed on the steps of Greyfriars Kirkyard while filming for his channel. The killer had not taken the camera and gimbal.

Robertson waited for him as McKenzie parked his vehicle in the NCP carpark on King Stables Road. "The death was called in by someone from the kirk."

"Did he have anything with him besides his filming equipment?" The DI clicked his key fob, locking the car, and lifted the collar on his overcoat against the wind, as cold snow stung his neck.

"Only a small camera bag, as far as we know," Robertson answered, herself wrapped in a cream hat and scarf; gloved hands pushed into the pockets of her long duck-egg blue coat. "Just to warn you, there's a sizeable crowd gathered at the cordon, and someone tried to get through it earlier to see the body... Said he was a fan."

"Christ!" McKenzie grimaced at what he considered a ghoulish fascination. "Can they not watch it on the news? It's too cold to be standing around gawking in this weather."

The snow crunched beneath their feet as large white flakes continued to swirl around them.

"Don't knock it, Grant." Susan walked ahead of him. "We need their input. The more interested they are, the more help we get."

It took around five minutes to arrive at the steps and go under the cordon. A large white tent covered the scene, its entrance busy with plastic-suited personnel coming and going. Emergency vehicles lined the street in both directions.

The detectives donned protective clothing and over-shoes and entered the tent.

The victim had fallen down the steps almost to the street, and lay in a crumpled heap, knees close to his chest, arms above his head as though he had held them out to break his fall. The body was wet from melted snow. Blood had run down the bottom steps and pooled on the pave-ment. It had mixed with the salt put down to keep the route clear of snow. Arterial spatter stained the base of the right-hand pillar at the entrance. Someone had walked through the crime scene, leaving slushy bloody footprints up the steps and a short way along the gritted path.

The DI pressed his lips together, swallowing as he assessed the scene. "He's not a small guy," he said to Susan, referring to the man's muscular frame. "It's a confident killer who attacks a man this size. Our victim was a gym-goer, I'd say."

"According to his blog, he worked out every morning," Robertson agreed.

"A confident killer with a very sharp knife." McKenzie knelt near the victim's head and lifeless hazel stare. "His mouth and eyes are open. Taken by surprise."

"And, like Margaret McLean, nobody reported hearing anything. No scream and no shouting."

Grant nodded. "He didn't know his killer was there. The murderer would not have risked being seen by the victim before he could attack. There are few who could win a fight against a guy this strong."

"Agreed."

"You say he was a true crime sleuth?" The DI stood. "Did he have a large following?"

"He had around one hundred thousand subscribers." Susan nodded. "I didn't have time to investigate further. We'll know more when we get back. But I would bet he was looking into the death of Margaret McLean. I'd put money on that being the reason he was here."

"And the killer struck after we removed the last officers from scene watch at the cemetery."

"Aye... Helen said she would make sure we have any CCTV footage from the street, and the church is going to check their cameras, in case the killer went farther up the kirkyard."

"Good. We should go along to the Greyfriars Bobby pub, in case their punters saw anything last night."

"We think he was killed around midnight," a SOCO looked up from his work. "He's still in rigor."

"When was he found?" Grant frowned.

"We got the call about six-thirty this morning. Did you

not see breakfast news?"

McKenzie shook his head. "We're always busy with kids, first thing." He thought about his wife. She usually took their children to school, but he made sure he helped her get their breakfast, get them dressed, and find any items they either needed or had lost. It was always hectic. Breakfast news was a luxury saved for weekends. "I think a guy from the kirk found him. A Tom... Tom..." The technician struggled to remember the name.

"Tim Shaw?"

"Aye, that was it. Tim Shaw."

"Thanks." The DI looked at Susan. "I say we start with him."

"Agreed." She nodded. "Brace yourself, it is baltic out there."

They made their way along the path to the kirk, Susan grabbing Grant's arm for particularly icy patches.

Snow continued to fall from a monotonous-grey sky as they entered Greyfriars Kirk.

Susan took off her hat, tucking it under one arm.

Grant brushed damp snow from the top of his head.

"Can I help you?" A portly woman in her fifties approached them from the noticeboards; holding fresh-cut flowers.

The DI held up his badge. "DI McKenzie, and DS Susan Robertson. We're looking for Tim Shaw. Is he around?"

"Oh, you must be here about the..." She stopped short of saying murder. "I'll go get him. He's had a bit of a shock. I'll only be a minute."

"We'll wait." Grant nodded, appreciating the refuge from the wind and snow. He walked over to browse the noticeboard, accompanied by the DS. It was populated mostly by news of upcoming events and concerts.

"How can I help?" Shaw's voice came from behind.

The DI turned to see the man dressed almost exactly as he had last seen him. The jumper was thicker, but was the same colour as the thinner one. "Mr Shaw." McKenzie walked towards him. "Is there somewhere we can go?"

"Yes, of course. Come through to our little office. We can talk in there."

The rest room for staff and volunteers was a modest yet relaxing space which carried the barely perceptible scent of aged wood and old books.

A large wooden table provided space for writing and eating, while the walls contained a few well-placed plaques, photographs, and artefacts reflecting the kirk's chequered history.

Shaw motioned for them to take a seat. His face had reddened, and his forehead appeared damp. "Had to nip out to give instructions to a volunteer caretaker," he said, as though aware of the DI's scrutiny. "I asked him to keep well away from the crime scene."

"Thank you." McKenzie took out his notebook. "I understand you found the body?"

"Yes..." Shaw ran a hand through his hair, his face lined with angst. "I thought at first it was a snow flurry. I was about to get a shovel to clear it when I realised there might be a person under there. It took me a few moments to work out what was going on. I thought someone had fallen asleep under the snow."

"What time was that?"

"Oh, it would have been a few minutes past six." Shaw took off his glasses to clean them, using breath and the bottom of his jumper.

"So, around five-past six?"

"About that time, yes."

"You phoned emergency services at six-thirty."

"Did I?" He put his spectacles back on.

Grant stopped writing to make eye contact with Shaw. "That is the official time logged. Why the delay?"

Tim frowned. "I didn't realise there was a delay. It didn't seem like that to me. I initially froze in shock at finding him there. I mean, I scraped back the snow a bit to see who it was. Then I ran to the church to make the call. But my hands were shaking, and I was cold. I was actually shivering from finding the body, and the being in the wind and snow. I couldn't dial right away. It took me a few minutes to warm up enough to use my phone. I didn't have it on me when I found him. I had left it in here, in my jacket pocket."

"Did you speak to anyone else when you found the victim?"

"I don't remember talking to anyone until after making the call. That's when I spoke to Joan, the lady who greeted you earlier. Joan Paterson is one of our volunteers. She helps with putting out bibles, arranging the flowers, and changing the notices. That sort of thing. She comes here several times a week. Her help is invaluable. I don't know what I would do without her. She arrived just after I did. That was before the police and ambulances got here."

"You say you didn't realise right away that you had stumbled on a murder victim."

"No... I did not know what I had found. I saw a shape covered in snow. I was approaching the steps. As I got closer, I realised there could be a person under the snow, and it wasn't simply a flurry from the blizzard. Snow had been piling up here and there, and it was difficult to tell the difference at first."

"Were you here yesterday?"

"I was."

"What time did you leave?"

"I guess it would have been around eight o'clock yesterday evening. I left a little later than planned. The last of the volunteers left around quarter to eight. That was Martin Ross. And I tidied around a bit before leaving."

"So, this guy Martin Ross... He left before you?"

"Aye. The killer wouldn't have wanted to mess with him."

"Oh? Why?"

"He's an ex-veteran. Two tours of Afghanistan. He's had his problems, mind. He struggled with drugs for a while and spent a few months on the streets. We helped him with food banks and got him accommodation. He's been popping in to help us ever since."

"A veteran, you say?" The DI made notes.

"Aye."

"And what time did you arrive home?"

"I got back to Dean Village around quarter-past or twenty-past eight, give or take."

"Can anyone corroborate that?"

"Can anyone... Wait, you don't think I had something to do with that man's death, do you?"

"Did you recognise the victim?"

"No."

"Had you seen him before?"

"Not that I recall."

"Did anyone see you arrive home? Do you live with anyone?"

"No, I live alone. My ex-wife and I divorced four years ago, and I have been single since then. I didn't see anyone when I got home. Does that make me a suspect?"

"We saw footprints in the snow that had traces of blood in them. Were they yours?"

"They could have been, yes. Like I told you, I came across the body before realising what it was. I walked very close to it. The footprints are most likely mine. I had covered over the victim by the time Joan arrived. She avoided the area."

"An officer will be along to examine your treads, so we know which prints are yours. Do you have alternative footwear?"

"Aye, I have a pair of trainers under there." He pointed to an alcove in the corner. "I'll put them on and leave my shoes in a carrier."

"Had anyone been to the kirk prior to yourself this morning?"

Shaw shook his head. "No."

"What about last night? Was anyone else in the church when you left?"

"No, I was alone after Martin went home."

"Did you see the victim in the kirkyard last night?"

"No, I didn't see anyone when I left."

"Could anyone else have come here after you locked the building?"

"Unlikely... Joan has a key, and the vicar and ushers have keys. But everyone signs in and out, and no-one signed in or out after I left. You can check the book. We lock the kirk of an evening, if we don't have an event on. I locked it when I left."

"And you have CCTV?"

"We do. An officer rang to ask us not to delete anything recorded by our cameras. Unfortunately, our system mainly focuses on the church, and not really on the kirkyard. But we don't have many visitors to the kirkyard after dark."

McKenzie nodded. "Someone will be here to collect the footage from you later this morning. If you are still here?"

"I must admit, I am a bit shaken up by all this and may go home soon. But I will ensure someone is here to give you what you need."

"We would appreciate that." McKenzie turned for the door.

"What do you make of him?" Susan asked as they headed back along the path towards the crime scene.

"I have a feeling he's not telling us everything he knows."

"He gives me the creeps." She glanced back towards the kirk. "Something about the way he moves and stares." She shuddered. "Do you not find him odd?"

"Aye, a little." Grant nodded. "Being odd doesn't make you a murderer, but he'll be on our suspect list until and unless we can rule him out. The volunteers sound interesting, too. That Martin Ross is worth checking out. Ex-veterans have knife skills. "

"Greyfriars pub was busy compared to his last visit. McKenzie suspected some patrons were in there to warm up after watching police activity near the kirk. He raised his voice for Susan to hear him above the chatter.

"I think that might be Pete Ramsey," he said of the man polishing pint glasses as they walked towards the bar.

"Pete Ramsey?" Susan didn't recognise the name.

"Aye, Gordon Caldwell told me that Ramsey was working the bar on the night Margaret McLean was murdered."

Robertson looked at the clean-shaven thirty-something

barman, with dark hair in a short ponytail at the back of his head, reminiscent of the Welsh footballer Gareth Bale. "I haven't seen him before."

"No, he's new. He started working here a couple of months ago. Works three nights a week and occasionally does days. I'm glad he's here. We really need to talk to him."

They found two spare bar stools, where they perched until Ramsey had a minute.

He looked over. "What can I get you?" he asked, his expression open.

"Are you Pete Ramsey?" Grant held up his badge. "We're from MIT in Leith. We were hoping to ask you a few questions."

Ramsey's brown eyes popped. "Me?"

"Aye, don't look so scared. I don't bite unless my wife hasn't fed me breakfast. We're here to talk to you about a woman who came in here last week. The lady who was murdered in the kirkyard, name of Margaret McLean."

Ramsey swallowed. "Aye, she came in here the night she was.... Well, you know." He blinked, rubbing the back of his neck. "She sat there for a while. He pointed to a table close to the bar. She mostly kept to herself. One guy sitting at the bar tried to make polite conversation with her, but she seemed engrossed in whatever she was reading, and I got the impression she wasn't interested in having a conversation." He cleared his throat, scanning the DI's face, trying to read his thoughts.

"You've not been working at the pub long then, eh?" McKenzie returned the stare. "I was in here talking to Gordon the other day. He said you work a few nights a week?"

"Aye... I'd like to go full time, but can't get the hours just now. I do extra shifts when other staff can't make it in. In fact, I wasn't meant to be working on the night that lass was murdered."

Grant's eyes narrowed. "You shouldn't have been here that night?"

"Gordon called me in the afternoon to ask if I could cover his shift that evening. I needed the money, so I said yes."

"Did he tell you why he couldn't do the shift himself?"

Ramsey thought about it. "Er, no he didn't. But I didn't ask."

"I see... Aside from thinking she was busy, did you notice anything else about Miss McLean?"

"She kept looking towards the door, like she was waiting for someone or she had to know who was coming in."

"Did she look fearful?"

"Not really... More watchful, I would say. I mean, I didn't see concern in her face. But she was definitely taking notice when people came in."

"You paid her a lot of attention, eh?"

Ramsey shrugged. "She was pretty, and on her own. I guess I was curious."

"Is there anything else you remember about that night?"

"No, nothing else."

"And you were behind the bar all night?"

"I was, aside from when I needed a leak. I was right here until just gone midnight."

McKenzie pushed a card over the bar to Ramsey. "That's our number. Call us if you remember anything else."

"Aye, I will."

GRAHAM AND HELEN were hard at work when Grant and Susan arrived back at Leith station.

"How's it going?" the DI asked.

Graham pushed his swivel chair back from his desk, turning to face them. "We've got nothing we can use from CCTV. No-one we could say was the killer. But we've had a few calls from TV stations and newspapers. I put them through to Sinclair."

"Good."

"And our murderer has a name now, apparently."

Grant raised a brow. "Really?"

"Aye... They're calling him The Gimbal Killer, on account of him murdering people making videos for social media."

The DI tutted. "So, not the Kirkyard Killer, then? That would have more of a ring to it, surely?"

"But Tam Fleming was killed in Dean Village."

"Are they tying his death in with McLean's and MacDonald's already? They've almost caught up with us."

"They are running a piece about Margaret McLean investigating Fleming's killing. They've been watching her YouTube videos."

"Aye, of course they have. Can you do me a favour, Graham?"

"Aye, what you after?"

"Can you set up an appointment for me with Gordon Caldwell from the Greyfriars Bobby pub? Tell him there are a few details I want to discuss with him."

"Have you got your eye on Caldwell?"

"He didn't tell me he took time off from the bar at short notice the night McLean was murdered. Don't tell him I know that. I want to see his reaction when I put it to him."

"Aye, no problem. Leave it to me."

7

TRUTH AND LIES

Forty-three-year-old Martin Ross sat across from DI McKenzie and DC Dalgliesh. He wore a formal shirt and jacket, without a tie. The jacket appeared two sizes too big for his lean frame. But strong biceps stretched the fabric of the upper arms. He had evidently had his dark hair trimmed recently and was wearing aftershave. His cheeks were shadowed and sunken, but the eyes were alert and bright. A forty-eight hour stubble peppered his prominent chin.

"Thank you for coming in, Mr Ross," the DI began. "You'll be wondering why we asked to see you?"

"Och, I assumed it was to ask me about the murders in the kirkyard." He pushed his hands into his trouser pockets, leaning back in his chair, appearing relaxed. "Because I volunteer there," he added.

McKenzie looked over his notes. "Tell me about that."

"The murders? Or the volunteering?"

"Do you know anything about the murders?"

"No."

"Then tell me about the volunteering. What do you do at the church, and how did you get started?"

"I was on the streets when I met the folks at the kirk. It was a couple of Christmases ago. They brought hot food and drinks for all of us on the street. They talked to me and took an interest. We're usually invisible out there. They treated us like human beings and, let me tell you, I needed their kindness."

"How long had you been homeless?"

"About three months. I was a lost soul... That's what they said."

"And you were using substances?"

"Drugs? Aye, I was. I'd been using Ketamine, and I went onto crack. The church helped me get off all of that. They made me feel appreciated, and like I wasn't alone. They got me looking at things differently."

"And you are ex-army?"

"I am. I was in the Royal Marines and did several tours of Afghanistan. Messed me up a bit. One of my mates lost his legs and tackle when an IED blew up in front of him. I had bits of him all over me. I helped save his life while we were waiting for CASEVAC."

"CASEVAC?"

"Aye, it's short for casualty evacuation."

"Right."

"My wife cheated on me and we split up while I was still serving. She stopped me from seeing my three-year-old while I was living on the streets. I had left the army by then, but had nowhere to go. The army encourages you to think about the future, and invest some of your wages or get a mortgage so you have something set up for when you leave. But my wife and I were renting, and I didn't expect us to split up. I didn't know I would exit the forces before retirement, so I didn't plan for it. What happened was my own fault in the end, but I went to pieces. I was angry with everyone, especially my ex-wife, while I was on the drugs. Volunteering helped me focus on other things, and the church got me a flat in Casslebank. It's close enough that I can get to the church by bus or walking."

"You don't own a vehicle?"

"No."

"Do you own knives?"

Ross's eyes narrowed. "Only for cooking."

"When did you leave the army?"

"June of twenty-twenty-one."

"When you left the Kirk on Sunday night, I understand Tim Shaw was still there?"

"Aye, he was. But he told me he would leave soon after I went."

"Did you see anyone else as you were leaving?"

"Not that I recall."

"But you would remember seeing someone?"

"Aye, I guess. I remember it being dark and silent when I left. There were one or two people walking on the street outside, but that's about it."

"What time would you say you left the Kirk?"

"Around nine."

"And where did you go?"

"I walked home."

"You didn't hang around the kirkyard for a while?"

"Do you think I had something to do with that man, James MacDonald, or his murder?"

"You know his name?"

"Aye, of course I know his name. He's been all over the news for the last two days. I thought nothing would take the limelight off the woman's murder at the kirk. Then the man was killed. Now they are both on top of the news."

"Does that make you angry?"

"It makes me annoyed that after all the kirk's good work, it gets tarnished with this kind of stuff. I feel sorry for those people that were murdered, but they shouldn't have been poking around like that, and spouting all that nonsense on YouTube. It was giving the kirk a bad press."

"Was it?"

"I thought so."

"But you hadn't heard of their YouTube channels before their deaths, so I'm surprised you became irritated by it after someone murdered them."

"Aye well, Mr Shaw was a bit upset by their antics, too. He said so."

"Did he?"

"Aye. I don't think he was happy they were murdered in the kirkyard. There was a lot of disruption from people coming and going afterwards... Police, journalists, and members of the public. Some services and events had to be cancelled. More events are due to be cancelled, too. There should have been a choir performance the night MacDonald was killed. They cancelled that one because of the woman's murder and the police inquiry."

"Had you seen either of the victims before? I mean, had you met them prior to their murders?"

"No, of course not. I heard of them only after they were killed, and I couldn't believe what they had been trying to do. I mean, who messes about in a kirkyard after dark, anyway? Anything could happen. And all because they thought they could solve crimes best left to the police. Madness, I call it."

"How long did it take you to get home on Sunday night?"

"I'm not sure... It was definitely by ten, I would say. I went to bed at eleven after I had a bite to eat and a bit of telly. By then, I was shattered."

"Did anyone see you arrive home?"

"No."

"How can you be sure?"

"I didn't see anyone else. I passed a few people on the way, but not when I got back to the flat. There was no-one about."

"What shoes were you wearing that night?"

"These." He lifted his feet below the table. "I only have one pair."

"Before you leave, we would like to take imprints of your shoes."

"Aye, all right. Am I free to go?"

"For now... I would like you to remain here for another few minutes, if you would. An officer will be along to take you to another room to get the shoe prints. Okay?"

Ross checked his watch. "Fine."

"HE'S STILL GOT some anger in him, eh?" Dalgliesh whistled through his teeth. "He's a wee bit like a bottle of pop. I wouldn't want to be on his bad side."

"He has the skills to commit murders like those of our victims. And a motive if he didn't like what they were doing and if he was lying to us about not knowing about them beforehand. But was his concern about the impact of the influencers' activities on the kirk enough of a reason for him to commit murder?"

FIFTY-EIGHT-YEAR-OLD DARREN PATERSON was the other volunteer mentioned by Shaw, who was due to be interviewed in Leith station. The volunteer had a pronounced cough over the phone, which he told Helen McAllister was the aftermath of a cold. He told her he was happy to attend for questioning, but doubted he could contribute anything useful.

"Mr Paterson." McKenzie was the last one to enter the room as DC Dalgliesh sat opposite the interviewee, making polite conversation until the DI was ready.

"Will this take long? I'm due at the kirk at four o'clock."

Grant checked his watch. It was ten-past-three. "We should be able to get this done in thirty or forty minutes. Will that be okay?" He noted Paterson's smart-casual appearance in cords, white shirt, and a blue country jacket with a tartan interior. He was around five-feet-eleven with a slim-to-medium build.

"Aye, should be." Darren took a glasses case out of his coat pocket. "I'll just put these on," he said.

McKenzie finished arranging his papers. "How long have you been helping at Greyfriars?"

"A few years now. I had a break from it last year because of a bout of sciatica, but got back into it once I was well enough."

"And what sort of things do you do there?"

"A bit of weeding, tidying of the graves and monuments, and I help with the choir and arranging furniture for events. That sort of thing."

"Are you happy with the work?"

"Aye, it keeps me occupied. I was getting a wee bit bored after I retired from teaching."

"Oh, aye? What did you teach?"

"Maths. The most popular subject." He grinned. "Not."

McKenzie laughed. "I have to confess, it wasn't my favourite in school."

"Well, I retired early when I was eligible for my pension at fifty-five, as I wanted a rest from the mayhem. But I was bored rigid after only a few months. My wife, Joan, was up to all sorts. Hobbies galore, she has. She suggested I help at the kirk, as they were looking for people and she was already helping there twice a week. I agreed, and the rest is history. I'm still there three years later."

"I admire your dedication," Grant flicked through his notes.

"Have you ever had concerns about anyone there?"

"In what way?"

"The kirkyard has a bit of a reputation around people getting injured."

"Oh aye, the old George 'Bloody' MacKenzie legend. Well, nothing's ever happened to me or my wife. I sometimes wonder if folks do it to themselves for attention. We used to get that sort of behaviour sometimes at the school."

"But they don't kill themselves for attention, do they?"

Paterson blanched. "That was a nasty business. That wasn't something we ever expected to see near the kirk."

"It must have come as a shock?"

"You don't think anybody at Greyfriars was involved in any of that, do you? No-one I know would harm a hair on anyone's head."

McKenzie held up a hand. "We are not accusing anyone. But we are wondering whether the killer may have involved himself with Greyfriars so he could learn the habits of those coming and going. We think the murderer knew exactly when to strike. He knew when he was least likely to be seen by anyone, and how to avoid being caught on the few CCTV cameras that exist in the area. The only footage we have is of those expected to be in the area."

"I see. Do you have any idea who did it? Are we in danger? The rumour is he attacked those youngsters because of what they were putting on social media. Their videos made someone unhappy, and he took his revenge out on them."

"Where did you hear that?" The DI leaned in.

"It's just what everybody is saying. I can't remember who said it, exactly. I heard a few people talking about it, though. And Joan told me yesterday that she had heard that story too, in other circles. She is a member of a historical society here, and she does coffee mornings and helps with a local food bank. She said people believe the victims were murdered because of what they knew."

"Did she say what it was they thought the victims knew?"

"Only that the victims were armchair detectives who had been investigating serious assaults and murder, and that they found things out they were not supposed to know."

"You can't be more specific than that?"

Paterson shook his head. "I'm sorry, I can't. I'm not really one for gossip. You know what the rumour mill is like... It's probably a load of old bunkum, anyway. Maybe they were just in the wrong place at the wrong time?"

"They were in a kirkyard."

"Aye, but it has a reputation for poltergeist activity, and they were there after dark. I think the guy was murdered around midnight. I guess he wanted to impress followers with his bravery. But I don't think it was the best decision in the world. The city can be a dangerous place at night."

"Evidently... You say you do a bit of weeding and general tidying at the kirkyard. Had you noticed anyone coming and going, maybe at odd times? Someone who, perhaps, might not have a reason to do so? Or anyone acting suspiciously?"

"No, I haven't. No-one that rang alarm bells with me, anyway. I mean, we get visitors to the kirkyard: tourists, history buffs, paranormal groups. We even get people filming in the kirkyard during the day for history channels. But, aside from the paranormal guys, we rarely have many filming at night. And when they come, there are usually several of them together. Safety in numbers, so to speak. We don't see anyone else, unless there is some event on at the kirk. Joan and I sometimes attend those evenings to help, or to watch as part of the audience. It's a popular place is Greyfriars."

"Where was your wife when you left the kirk?"

"She was at home. She hadn't been at Greyfriars all day. It wasn't her day to help."

"Had you seen either of the victims at the graveyard before?"

Paterson shook his head.

"Had you ever spoken to them or interacted with them?"

"No. When I saw their faces on TV, I didn't recognise them at all."

"If you hear anything else about the deaths, you'll let us know?"

"Aye, straight away."

"Good... Be careful when you are out and about. Tell your wife, too. Until we catch this killer, we would advise against walking alone in the area after dark."

"I'll let Joan know. She wouldn't want to walk on her own after dark, anyway, but it doesn't hurt to remind her."

"Thank you, Mr Paterson. We'll see you out."

～

GORDON CALDWELL LOOKED DIFFERENT; less burly somehow, when he wasn't behind the bar.

McKenzie was interviewing him by himself, having left the others with multiple tasks to get on with. He showed the Greyfriars Bobby barman in, pulling out a chair for him to sit at the table in the middle of the soundproofed room.

Caldwell took off his jacket, undid the top button on his shirt, and rolled his sleeves up.

The DI could smell the damp heat coming off him. "Are you okay, Gordon?" He eyed the other man's red face.

"Aye, I thought I was going to be late. I ran all the way here from the car park. It took me a full five minutes to get my breath back. I'm not as fit since I gave up playing football for the pub team. It's surprising how quickly you go downhill when you dunnae get off your ass as much."

Grant grinned. "I don't have that luxury. I am always chasing some rum beggar down the street."

"Aye, you keep yourself pretty fit, eh? I notice some police officers putting on the weight, but not you."

"My kids keep on my toes, never mind the criminals. I've always got my hands full."

"So, what am I doing here? I assume it's about the murders?"

"Aye... Did you do them?"

"What?" Caldwell's mouth hung open.

The DI grinned, but his eyes were watchful. "I'm just kidding with you, maybe."

Caldwell puffed out his cheeks. "For a minute there, I thought you were serious."

"For a minute, so did I."

Caldwell studied McKenzie's face, his brow furrowed. "Why am I here?" he asked.

"You're here to help us with our enquiries." Grant felt

torn. Unnerving the barman made it more likely he would slip up if he was guilty. But Caldwell was more than an acquaintance. Over the last few years, they had become friends. The barman had supplied crucial intelligence in two former inquiries.

"I thought I had given you what I know?"

"You did, but there was something you neglected to tell me."

The barman shrugged, his face a mask, but he swallowed hard. "I can't think what that would be."

"You called Pete Ramsey on the afternoon of Margaret McLean's murder to ask him to cover your shift that night. It should have been you working in the bar, not Pete. Why did you cancel?"

"I guess I felt unwell."

"You guess? Surely you know if you were feeling sick?"

"I thought I was coming down with something, as I didn't feel quite right. I called Pete, in case it got worse."

"Where were you that evening?"

"At home."

"Not at the kirkyard?"

"Why would I be at the kirkyard?"

"Margaret McLean updated her social media that morning to let her followers know she intended filming at the kirk that night. She knew the risk she was running, and that suggests to me she was looking to lure the attacker."

"And you think her target was me? That I am the person she was trying to bait? What would *I* want with hurting anyone? Or with killing them? Why would I have wanted her dead?"

"I'm not saying you did, Gordon. I'm just asking the question."

"I thought we were pals. Or we got on well, at least."

"It's not personal." McKenzie sighed, taming his hair when it fell onto his face. "Everyone is a suspect until we rule them out, especially those who knew the victim and were in the area."

"Och, I hardly knew the girl. She popped into the pub to write some notes. And she wasn't there for very long. It was quite clear she had work to do and focussed on doing it. And that wasn't personal, either."

"You said Pete Ramsey covered for you."

"Aye, he did."

"The way you were talking there, it seemed like you were relating first-hand experience."

"I'm telling you in the way Ramsey told me, in case you think she went there to meet up with me or something."

"Did she?"

"No."

"Folk in the pub that night said she looked like she was watching for someone; looking over at the door now and then."

"I wouldn't know about that."

"Are you sure?"

"Look, this is harassment. You can't bring me in here and start accusing me of stuff."

"I'm not accusing, I'm asking you."

"Aye, all right. But I'm telling you, no... to all of what you said. None of it is right."

McKenzie's gaze lowered to his papers, his head still; the silence in the interview room was tangible.

"Can I ask you something?" Caldwell snapped back in his chair.

"Of course." Grant's steady gaze gave nothing away.

"Did you ask me in here because you really believe I had

something to do with those murders? Or because you think I may know who did?"

"I wanted to talk to you again, because you took the day off from work, the day of Margaret McLean's murder, at short notice. And because she visited your pub, possibly looking for someone, before her killer murdered her. I wanted to know if the person she sought was you."

"Well, now you have your answer."

"Then we can conclude the meeting." McKenzie tidied and stacked his papers.

Caldwell frowned. "Really?"

"Yes."

"I can go, then?"

"You can."

The barman opened and closed his mouth before grabbing his jacket from the back of the chair. "Right... I'll be off."

The DI didn't look up from his papers. "Take care, especially near the kirkyard at night."

The door clicked shut.

McKenzie was unsure if Caldwell was being truthful, but had nothing concrete to suggest the barman had known Margaret McLean. He needed to dig deeper into Margaret's investigations, beginning with the death of Tam Fleming, though he would first have to face the furore that would surely come with the murder of James McDonald, the second of the kirkyard victims. McDonald's killing had happened on their watch. While the team had concentrated on what they thought was a one-off, targeted murder, the killer had coolly slipped back to take another victim. Truth be told, the DI was having a hard time forgiving himself for that. But it made him even more determined to get to the heart of whatever was going on in this case.

8

TAM FLEMING

It took precisely twenty minutes to travel from Greyfriar's Bobby to the picturesque Dean Village, nestled along the water of Leith. The place seemed woven from the tapestry of time itself; each step along its narrow lanes like a journey through the pages of a classic novel. Cobblestoned streets wound through an enclave steeped in beautiful, historic architecture, and a collection of quaint stone houses that whispered of former centuries. It offered a serene escape and refuge from the bustling city, transporting its visitors to an almost timeless realm.

Ancient mill buildings, once the heartbeat of industry, were now silent witnesses to the bygone era. Moss-covered stone bridges arched gracefully over gentle water, connecting the village to the world outside.

McKenzie had ridden the number twenty-seven bus from the same stop where Tam Fleming had waited for his ride the year before. The rising true-crime influencer, with over one hundred thousand followers, was attacked while making a selfie video on his way home. The hapless young man, immersed in filming-making, lost his life in the yellow glow of street lamps as he awaited his transport home.

As the DI discovered, the bus journey to Dean Village would have taken precisely twenty minutes. Although not a crucial detail in the murder timeline, McKenzie travelled the route to better understand the victim's routine. Whoever killed Fleming had likely also familiarised themselves with it.

Tam met his untimely demise as he held his mobile phone on a gimbal, filming near the Greyfriars Bobby. He had spent the previous hour in Greyfriars Kirkyard, doing the same. CCTV at the time recorded a masked figure walking along the street. The attacker took a sharp detour before taking out the twenty-nine-year-old victim. This had made it look like a spur-of-the-moment robbery gone wrong; the victim making a futile attempt at fighting off the killer. By the time the bus pulled up, Fleming had lost his battle for life, and passengers looked on helplessly as emergency services arrived. The victim's gimbal was still in his hand. Two men, who had committed another armed robbery that night, were convicted for Tam's death after they used his chip and pin at a supermarket. McKenzie suspected the actual killer was still out there.

According to her notes, Margaret McLean had been following up on Tam's work; geographically profiling sexual assaults committed in the Greyfriars area. Geo-profiling was the forensic investigative technique used to analyse the spatial patterns between crimes, particularly serial crimes, to determine the likely base or anchor point of the offender. It relied on the assumption that criminals often commit offences near their home or workplace, creating a pattern whose analysis enabled educated predictions about the likely residence or operational centre of the offender.

One of Fleming's few remaining videos showed him attempting to triangulate the suspect's location, based on assaults committed within the kirkyard and beyond. Mckenzie watched the video with Margaret's maps and notes in front of him. She had taken Tam's information and added more of her own, concentrating on a ten-mile radius from Greyfriars, where three of the attacks had occurred. Other locations she had plotted included Edinburgh Castle, Princes Street Gardens, Carlton Hill, St. Margaret's Loch, and even the Royal Mile. Greyfriars was the site of three assaults.

Although not enamoured with civilians trying their hand at police work, because of the inherent risk involved, Margaret and Tam's work impressed the DI. The two influencers had put in a great deal of effort and taken their investigations seriously. They had clearly worked hard to nail down the attacker and had evidently scared him into taking them both out, if Grant's suspicions were correct. Had the killer watched Tam and Margaret's videos? McKenzie thought it likely.

As he viewed the red-haired, bright-eyed Margaret McLean talk to her followers about her work, he found it hard believing the woman he viewed on screen breathed no more. Her energy and enthusiasm were infectious, and she had rapidly built an impressive following, as had Fleming. Both influencers were convinced the killer was intimately linked with Greyfriars. The DI felt sure they were right.

"OUR KILLER IS in the papers again." Dalgliesh plopped the local rag down on McKenzie's desk.

"Is he?" Grant unfolded the paper to read the front-page

headline. 'Police in an increasingly desperate hunt for The Gimbal Killer,' it read.

"They mention you in there, by the way." Graham grinned. "Except they spelled your name wrong. Apparently, you are DI M-a-cKenzie now," he said, emphasising the extra vowel. "Just like good old Bloody-George himself."

"Oh, great..." The DI grimaced. "As long as they haven't portrayed me as some blood-thirsty psychopath running round the kirkyard wreaking my revenge on all and sundry, I can live with the odd misspelling or two."

"They've not said you're a blood-thirsty killer, but they have called you clueless."

"Clueless?" McKenzie put his hands on his hips, mock outrage on his face.

"Aye, you ken what they're like... What they don't know, they make up as they go along. Apparently, you're 'clueless as to the person who committed the crime'."

"Is that so?" Grant pulled a face. "Cheeky bastards. If we haven't got the killer cuffed and sentenced within forty-eight hours, we should probably look for another job, eh?"

"Aye... On a positive note, we think we have MacDonald's killer captured on CCTV."

"You have? Great..." McKenzie leaned over his desk. "Can we see his face?"

Dalgliesh shook his head. "Unfortunately, not. It was snowing heavily the night MacDonald was murdered. A blizzard, in fact. The captured images are blurry, but they have gone to technicians at the lab to see what they can do about enhancing and clearing them up a bit. They might, at least, give us an estimate of the perpetrator's height and weight."

"That would be good if we could match it to one of our suspects. Are uniform watching the kirkyard?"

"Aye."

"Good. They better not take their eyes off it, though I doubt our perp will go near there for a while. Not for a killing, anyway..."

"Who's suspect number one?" Dalgliesh pushed his hands into his trouser pockets. "Are you still thinking Gordon Caldwell?"

McKenzie stood to examine the whiteboard. On it, the five people they were considering in relation to the murders. Andy Scott, Margaret McLean's partner; Martin Ross, a Greyfriars volunteer and former marine; Darren Paterson, also a volunteer at Greyfriars and who mainly worked in the kirkyard; Tim Shaw, the man who organised the volunteers, and was at the kirk all hours; and Gordon Caldwell, barman at the Greyfriars Bobby, who had called in sick last minute on the day of Margaret McLean's murder. Each had a reason to be in the area, but could also be the person at the centre of Tam Fleming's geo-profiled assaults.

The DI sighed. "Right now, Graham, I wouldn't like to say. We have a lot more to do. I want you and Helen to dig into the sex attacks mentioned in these papers." He handed some of Tam and Margaret's notes to the DC. "And cross-check the geo-profiling. I think these kids were onto something. They were close enough to scare the perpetrator into taking them out. I believe Tam Fleming's killing is linked to Margaret's and James's murders. Are you okay to check them out?"

"Aye, leave it with me. I'll get into it with Helen this afternoon. What are you going to do?"

McKenzie checked his watch. "Oh hell, I'm supposed to be at the mortuary." He grabbed his coat. "Will you be all right with what I've given you?"

"Aye, you get off. We'll be fine." Dalgliesh grabbed the papers and headed for the door. "Give Fiona my best."

the case, for him to say a few words." Sinclair moved away from the podium after giving Grant the nod.

McKenzie swallowed, realising he should have been listening so as not to repeat anything the DCI had said. He mentally shrugged. If he did, it would be tough luck.

He outlined the work they had done, and the numbers of witnesses they had interviewed, without being too specific. Before he handed the podium back to Sinclair, however, he cast a serious gaze over all present. "We believe this killer has his eyes on social media, specifically on true crime influencers who are sleuthing Edinburgh crimes. I hope all reporters present will include a warning in their write-ups today for those individuals, reminding them of the dangers of filming on location. The killer could strike while they are distracted. We want no more victims added to the list. I would extend the warning to yourselves, too, when investigating these crimes. Keep your wits about you, especially after dark, and when on location. Thank you."

McKenzie was about to step back from the lectern when Sinclair raised a hand, to say he had to go. That meant the DI would have to stay where he was, fielding questions from the floor. He lost count of the number of times he said they couldn't be more specific on a particular point for fear it might compromise the investigation. Let them call him clueless. It was better than giving the killer a heads up. When he finally finished, it was a ragged version of himself who left the podium. Glad the conference was over, he cursed Sinclair under his breath for slinking off.

10

UNSUSPECTING PREY

The young woman wandered down the aisle on autopilot as her eyes scanned items on the shelves. Occasionally, one wheel of her trolley froze and she would jerk the handle to get it moving again. Shoulder-length clumps of sandy hair fell loose from a clip that was trying to hold it in a bun, probably inserted in haste before she left the house. Each time the cart stuttered, she acted with increasing frustration. He could feel irritation oozing from her pores like sweat.

He turned his head. She almost caught him that time. Almost discovered him looking at her; weighing her up. She would be easy. She couldn't be over five-foot-two, and that was being generous. He looked at her shoes. Had to be a good couple of inches on those, at least. She wouldn't film in that pair. They never did. She would wear flats to make her videos among the Edinburgh streets and parks. He would have the advantage, like those with air superiority in a battle. Victory would be all but certain. The Goliath to her David, except she had no slingshot, and therefore couldn't win.

The young woman looked over cereals, pulling boxes forward to read the ingredients or calorie content, and pushing them back *before grabbing another. She took her time deciding. He never shopped like that. He knew exactly what he wanted and where he wanted it from. There would be no milling about; pondering the whys and wherefores for him. Shopping with her would do his head in. Good job he wasn't in the market for a new girlfriend. He didn't need one to do what he wanted. He could take that for free. Perhaps she would stop for a beer, its effects making the eventual ambush easier for him.*

The woman finally chose the box she wanted, tossing it into her cart and moving on down the aisle.

He disappeared from the supermarket before she reached the checkout. Today was only a reconnaissance.

ONCE THE CHILDREN had settled in bed, and Jane had cosied up on the sofa with a throw and her favourite drama, Grant gave her a kiss on the forehead before heading to the study. He wanted to know if there were more true-crime sleuths on YouTube, based in Edinburgh and, if so, whether the cases they were working on would interest The Gimbal Killer, causing him to seek those influencers out. He only found two: Carol Fraser and Giles Douglas.

Multiple thumbnails appeared for the unsolved cases they were working on. The DI watched a selection of them.

Carol's articulate narration painted a mysterious but vivid picture of each of her cases. The haunting way in which she delivered her narrative, mixed with particular outtakes of the Edinburgh streets, drew him in. Camera angles captured the city's eerie corners and alleyways, giving the viewer a sense of festered secrets, and of old buildings as silent witnesses to crimes unfolding in the dark. Each case dripped with unresolved tension, heightened by the perfect timing of the young woman's interjections. McKenzie ran a hand through his hair, worried that the influencer's pursuit of truth in the Greyfriars attacks, and Margaret McLean's murder, might have placed her in the crosshairs of the city's vicious and elusive killer. In her quest for justice, Carol Fraser could inadvertently have become a potential target.

For the last hour before bed, he immersed himself in the analytical world of the second sleuthing influencer, Giles Douglas, whose delivery was much more matter-of-fact. His videos unfolded like a procedural drama, each episode dissecting crime scenes with a meticulous attention to detail. The detective in McKenzie recognised the precision of Giles's assertions and deductions, a skill that would almost certainly make him an unwitting target for a killer hell-bent on remaining free to commit atrocious acts. The city, through Douglas's lens, transformed into a maniacal chessboard where every move had consequences. Grant wondered if the influencer knew that for him, personally, the stakes couldn't be higher.

Although the DI didn't yet have their ages, he thought Giles Douglas the older of the two, and estimated the YouTuber to be in his mid-thirties, while Carol Fraser looked to be around ten years younger. The DI yawned as he made notes on each, eyes watering from fatigue.

Once satisfied he had what he needed, McKenzie made his way to Jane and bed.

11

INFLUENCING INFLUENCERS

G rant and Susan navigated the cobblestone streets of Greyfriars, their destination the Georgian townhouse of social media sleuth Carol Fraser, who had been investigating sexual assaults and murders occurring in that part of the city. She lived in the house with two of her friends.

McKenzie rang the bell.

Carol opened the door, dressed in a tee shirt and joggers, and with a towel turban around her straw-coloured hair. She smelled of strongly scented soap and appeared more ordinary than the enigmatic woman the DI had seen on screen the evening before.

"Carol?" he asked.

"That's me, come on in. I'm sorry, I'm running a bit late," she said as she ushered them along the hallway to a shared lounge in a cream colour scheme with magenta accents provided by cushions and rugs. Two sash windows flooded the room with light. Unframed modern canvases dotted the walls.

"Is it okay to talk?" DS Robertson asked, before sitting on the couch.

"Yes... My friends are at work. I'm usually alone here during the day. I work for myself from home, so it's great... I need peace for the zillion things I have to do each day." She looked into an oval mirror above the mantlepiece, examining barely perceptible bags under hazel eyes. "God... Look at these." She turned to the detectives. "I hope you don't think I'm self-absorbed. It's just that studio lighting can be so unkind. Or, at least, mine can. I am doing a 'live' later," she said, referring to a livestream video. "Lives are popular with my audience. I don't think it's professional to have a washed-out look on my videos. Though I don't suppose anyone really cares."

Though he thought her somewhat neurotic, the DI appreciated her honesty and openness. It was refreshing when compared with some others they came across in their day-to-day. "I'm sure you'll be fine." He grinned. "It's never as bad as you think."

Carol smiled, her face relaxing. "You wanted to talk about my work?" she asked.

"Aye, I know DS Robertson spoke to you yesterday, but some things are best said in person."

"You've got me all intrigued." She rubbed her hair with the towel before getting up to place the latter on the radiator. Her damp, shoulder-length locks appeared more light brown rather than sandy-blonde.

The DI noticed how slight she was. She would be no match for the fiend stalking Greyfriars. "We advise you to take extra precautions when filming out and about for your channel."

"Do you mean because of The Gimbal Killer?" She pushed damp hair out of her face.

"Oh, good... You know of him." Susan Robertson nodded. "We think he attacks the people digging into serious crimes in the area. Particularly offences he has had involvement in."

"He strikes when his targets are filming within the city, particularly around the Greyfriars area," McKenzie agreed. "He likes them distracted."

"I made a video about him only last night." She grimaced. "I haven't edited it yet, so it's not ready for upload, but I had noticed a pattern, even without seeing the headlines."

"Do you have someone to accompany you when you are out and about?"

"I can ask my boyfriend, I guess. And there is a cameraman I use for some of my videos. I don't use him a lot, as his help doesn't come cheap and, although my channel is monetised, I barely make enough to live on. Hence why I am in shared accommodation at the age of twenty-six."

"We think he stalks his victims, sizing them up before striking. Keep your eyes open for anyone hanging around or following you, including in a vehicle."

Carol pulled a face.

"Have you noticed anyone lurking around here lately. Perhaps someone who keeps popping up, or that makes you feel uncomfortable?"

The influencer's eyes widened. "Oh God, you don't think... Has he been watching me already? I mean, me specifically? I don't really know what I expected, but I assumed The Gimbal Killer hung around the Old Town waiting to attack anyone who was filming or wearing head-phones, so they wouldn't have time to react. And so he wouldn't get into a scrap."

"Aye, we don't think that description is far off the mark, but we believe he stalks his victims for a while beforehand. It may be on social media, but it could also be in person. He seems to know where to strike, meaning he has a heads up regarding where and when his victims will film outdoors."

"You could set up a sting... I could be the bait." Her eyes lit up.

"We could..." Grant smiled at her enthusiasm. "But we are loath to put civilians in harm's way. If we did something like that, we'd be dangling a police officer in front of him, not a member of the public."

"Damn." Carol sighed. "Oh well, it was a thought. My subscribers would have loved it." She thought for a moment. "Maybe your officer could pretend to be me?"

"Aye, but... And I don't want to be alarmist here... If you are on his list, he'll already know what you look like." McKenzie pressed his lips together.

Carol swallowed. "Silly me... Of course he would."

"Were you planning on filming outside soon?"

"I was in two minds, actually. I thought about filming in the kirkyard, where Margaret and James were murdered, while your officers are still patrolling there. Not at night, though. I wouldn't be up for that. But, during the day, I'd be okay with police about, wouldn't I?"

Susan pulled a face. "Probably, but I personally wouldn't want to tempt either fate or this killer."

"Oh, I wouldn't go alone." Carol nodded. "I'd definitely have someone with me, even with the police about. My subscribers expect me to dive into the thick of things. I'm always drumming up new and exciting ways to keep them engaged. There's always an influencer out there who will do more. One-upmanship, you know?"

"Don't risk your life attempting to outdo your rivals. You can't compete if you're... Well, you know."

The young woman nodded. "I won't take unnecessary risks. I'll take all the precautions I can."

"Good." McKenzie moved to the edge of his seat, a glint in his eye. "While we're on the subject, do you have a suspect?"

Carol grinned. "Are you tapping me for ideas, DI McKenzie? I thought you guys would think me a pain-in-the-ass armchair wannabe."

"Aye, but we'd be nothing without the public's help. We appreciate any tips."

She pursed her lips, a reciprocal glint appearing in her own eyes. "Who is your favourite suspect? Do you have one?"

The DI laughed. "Nice try... Anyway, for all we know, it could be a rival sleuth who killed Margaret and James."

Carol paused, mouth open. "Wait, I hadn't thought of that."

"We'd better be off." Grant stood, checking his watch. "We have other appointments today."

"Thanks for the warning." She stood to see them out. "I'll let you know if I see anyone dodgy hanging about."

"Thank you, Miss Fraser."

AFTER LEAVING CAROL'S TOWNHOUSE, McKenzie and Robertson headed for Giles Douglas's home in a converted warehouse in the Edinburgh's Old Town, whose blackened bricks gave a nod to the city's industrial past.

They climbed the well-worn staircase to his door, which the DI gave a rap.

A barefoot young man opened it, wearing only shorts and a tee shirt. As Grant looked around, he realised the influencer must be doing well for himself. The decor was distinctly upmarket, with well-chosen pieces that sat comfortably in the space. The interior walls made bare-brick a feature, and large windows allowed light to pour in, giving the space a calming, airy feel. Douglas's home was almost exactly as the DI pictured it, after watching the amateur sleuth's analytical mind at work on video the night before. Everything was in its place. Shelves stood lined with fiction and non-fiction books on crime, arranged according to height and subject. A large, square pine table contained a laptop, pens, and notepads. And Giles had aligned everything in perfect parallel.

He led them to a black leather sofa and sat on the chair opposite. He offered them a drink, which they declined.

McKenzie took a moment to appreciate the view over the tenements below. "Thank you for agreeing to see us at such short notice," he began.

"No problem..." Giles shrugged. "I hadn't made plans to go anywhere today. I'm writing scripts and editing videos." Douglas ran a hand through dark hair containing salon-added blonde highlights. His chiselled chin bore a pronounced cleft, while high cheekbones and forehead rendered him a lofty, intellectual air. He looked the university type. His physique, and the gym equipment in one corner of the room, suggested he worked out daily.

"I'm sure you already know we are investigating the deaths of Margaret McLean and James MacDonald. They were fellow members of your true crime community and YouTube influencers like yourself."

He nodded, rubbing his hands together as though he

were cold. "It's the talk of the internet. I've not heard much else since they were killed."

"Is that where you heard about their murders? On the internet?" McKenzie took out his notebook.

Giles nodded. "Rumours abounded on the net before anything hit the news... They were talented investigators. I watched their videos frequently and learned a lot. We learn from each other in the true crime community. Everyone feeds into the melting pot of information. Though sometimes people poach each other's stuff, and that's not so good. There is friendly and unfriendly rivalry."

"I see." McKenzie made notes. "Has anyone ever stolen your work?"

Giles shrugged. "Occasionally, yeah, they have. Once or twice, I have had to tell people to take my stuff down, especially when they used my footage without attribution. That's the worst, when people do that."

"Were they from Edinburgh?"

"No, they were mostly from further afield. There are probably scores, if not hundreds, of us when you consider national and international channels. It's not unusual for true crime buffs in the US to report on UK crime, and vice versa."

"What about Margaret McLean and James MacDonald? How well did you know them?"

"I knew them reasonably well. I met them once."

McKenzie's steady gaze met Douglas's. "You did?"

"Oh yeah, we had a few beers in the Greyfriars Bobby."

"When was this?"

"Oooh, I think it was last spring; almost a year ago, now."

"Why did you get together?"

"We met up because we were interested in attacks happening in the Greyfriars area. We all felt that several cases were likely linked. A guy called Tam Fleming was killed not long before, and we met to discuss his geo-profiling work, and brainstorm the cases over a few bevvies. It was a great meet up. You can imagine my shock and sadness at learning about James's and Margaret's deaths."

"When did you first learn of their murders?"

"I knew of Margaret's the day after it happened, because I had been busy the previous night, and didn't see the rumours flying round on social media until the following morning. And James's death... I heard about the same day."

"How did you find out?"

"I saw the discussions on Facebook, and the news which I usually get from YouTube. It was all over my feed."

"But you hadn't logged into your social media on the day Margaret was killed?"

"No, I didn't log into Facebook at all on the day Mags died. I was filming on location earlier in the day and probably editing a video for my channel that evening. She was a really nice girl. Dedicated. Worked hard for her followers. She didn't deserve what happened to her."

"So, all three of you were aware of Tam Fleming's death and were interested in his geo-profiling?"

"Yes... Tam started out as an IT consultant for a large company in the city. He was involved in app development and was interested in algorithms. He was a natural at creating programs to do unusual tasks. So he made a geo-profiling app and used it for his true-crime cases. The stuff he did on the Greyfriars attacks was fascinating. After his death, we thought it would be useful to get together and go through his results."

"Did you wonder if it was Tam's work that got him killed?" McKenzie scoured Giles's face.

"Well, no. We thought he tried to fight off a mugger

armed with a knife and came of worst." The influencer scratched his head. "Are you saying he was killed because of his investigations? Like Mags and James?"

"We don't know, but it is something we are considering."

"Oh..." He glanced at his laptop. "That is interesting..."

"Did you see either Margaret or James again after meeting up that spring?"

Giles shook his head. "No... We had said we would, but then we never got around to it. I don't think any of us could have foreseen what would happen. If we had, it would have scared us witless. And now, the press thinks the killer is someone who attacks people who are preoccupied with phones or cameras."

"That is what they are reporting, yes."

"Is that what you think?"

McKenzie pressed his lips together before answering. "We think it is likely, Mr Douglas."

The influencer looked out over the houses. "Their murders put me off filming around the city. I mean, we don't know where he'll strike next, do we?"

"But you had Tam Fleming's geo-profiling data."

"Sure, but that was for the sexual assaults, wasn't it?"

"Oh, yes..." McKenzie gave a slow double-blink. "My mistake."

"It's easy to be confused. You have information coming at you all the time and from all angles. I wonder how you cope with it."

Was he fishing for information? The DI wasn't sure. "You let us worry about that. The more intel, the better as far as we are concerned. Any information is usually better than none."

"I'll keep my eyes and ears open... I do, anyway, because I have to. I'll let you know if I learn anything."

"Do that. In the meantime, be careful when you are out and about. We have three dead true-crime influencers. We don't want to find another one."

"I'll go canny. I'll be fine."

As GRANT and Susan walked to their vehicle, the DS turned to the DI. "Did you get a funny feeling about him? He's very smooth, don't you think?"

"Aye..." McKenzie unlocked the car with his fob. "We should keep a close eye on him. He obviously gets upset about others stealing his material. But did the victims take any of their footage from him, and could that be a motive for murder? It may be something for Helen and Graham to chase up. I have watched hours of true crime YouTube... I think it's their turn."

"JAMES MACDONALD..." Graham spun his chair round to face the returning duo.

"What about him?" McKenzie removed his overcoat. "What have you found?"

"His following was smaller than the other victims, but still pretty sizeable at two-hundred-thousand subscribers. His channel was monetised, but had only been going for twelve months, apparently."

"Really?" Grant frowned.

"Aye... a meteoric rise, no?"

"That seems fast to me."

"Well, it did to everyone else, too. I was reading the

comments on some of his videos, and there were a few raising eyebrows."

"What were they saying?"

"Some accused him of cheating his way to monetisation. He had received two strikes for copyright over the last three months of his life. And there were comments threatening to cause more. He was at risk of demonetisation or even losing his channel, they said."

"What was he alleged to have done? Stolen material from other influencers?"

"Aye, that's what they were saying. It got pretty heated, too. He used some of Tam Fleming's geo-profiling stuff without properly crediting the deceased creator. Some commenters really took exception to that..."

"Did you see similar things on Margaret McLean's videos? I started watching her material, but read none of the comments. As far as I could see, she credited Tam Fleming with the geo-profiling material. I can't really see her stealing other people's information intentionally, but it's possible she used footage and forgot to credit the source."

"I haven't found plagiarised material far, but I have only just begun going through the comments on her shows, and there's a lot of stuff to get through."

"Good work, Graham. And you read our minds... We discussed asking you to look into possible strife on the channels as we were driving back. Is Helen helping?"

"She is, and if you get your skates on, you'll catch her at the kettle for a brew."

Susan grinned. "Now you're talking."

12

AN INTRIGUING LINE

DCI Sinclair leaned back in his chair, eyeing McKenzie over steepled hands. Outside, the sky had darkened as storm clouds scudded over.

Tension in the DI's back and shoulders reflected his superior's impatience as Sinclair's eyes bored into him.

"When can you give me something on the kirkyard murders? I've got everybody waiting for this. You know Holyrood is paying attention. And it's affecting local tourism."

McKenzie stood firm. "I know it might not seem like it, but we are making progress. It's a painstaking process, you know that. We still have interviews to conduct, and we're working our way through them as fast as we can. The team is working hard, and I believe we'll have a breakthrough soon."

Sinclair drummed his fingers on the desk. "It doesn't get much more high profile than this. Because of who the victims were, and the numbers of followers they had online, we've got world-wide attention. I think Jack the Ripper himself would find it hard to compete with this case. Look, I understand the need for thoroughness, I do. But we can't afford to let this case go cold. And that is my worry. If this gets drawn out over the coming weeks, we'll lose impetus. The public is getting anxious. Holyrood is getting anxious. And the higher-ups are breathing down my neck. We need results, McKenzie. And we need them fast."

Grant rubbed his aching forehead. "We're doing everything we can, sir. This is a complex case which requires careful handling. We identified others at risk of becoming victims and have warned them. The team won't rest until we find this killer and bring him to justice. You must trust us to do our job. We have got this."

"And what do I tell the chief?"

"Tell him we are making progress, because we are. If he wants more? Say we are working on something we are not yet ready to disclose."

The DCI's brow furrowed. "Is that true?"

"Aye."

Sinclair sighed. "I expect updates, McKenzie. Keep me informed and get this case moving forward so it feels like we're getting somewhere. Lives are at stake, and I am sick of having my collar felt by those in charge."

"Leave it with us, Rob." McKenzie hoped his words sounded more confident than he felt, but Sinclair appeared happy with them, for now.

CAROL FRASER PAUSED HER NARRATIVE, to read the conversation unfolding on the chat of her livestream from viewers discussing her investigation into The Gimbal Killer on her YouTube channel.

SallyOne453: I Love your shows, Carol. I never miss one. Keep up the good work. Your channel is the best.

She appreciated the support from her viewers. No matter how many times she received it, it always lifted her heart and helped to keep her motivated.

CarolFr: Thank you so much, SallyOne453! I'm glad you enjoy my content.

SallyOne453: Your attention to detail is amazing. I think you are ahead of everyone else investigating this killer.

CarolFr: That's very kind, thank you, SallyOne.

SallyOne453: I don't know how you make the time. You pack your shows with so much.

CarolFr: Thank you.

The influencer would have left it there, turning her attention to other users in the chatroom. But the next line had the creator glued to the screen.

SallyOne453: I could tell you some things about this killer.

Carol leaned closer to her computer screen.

CarolFr: What do you mean? Do you know something? Feel free to share, SallyOne453.

SallyOne did not reply, and the chat moved swiftly on without her; the intriguing message becoming lost in the rapidly scrolling feed.

Carol's excitement turned to confusion as she scanned the text, searching for any further trace of SallyOne453.

CarolFr: Hey, SallyOne453, where did you go? If you have information about the Greyfriars murders, please come back!

Minutes passed, but SallyOne453 had gone. Concerned, Carol continued.

CarolFr: Seriously, if you have information about this case, please reach out. I'd love to talk.

The livestream continued, but without SallyOne. Carol couldn't shake the feeling the woman's sudden disappearance was because someone else had walked in on her. Perhaps the mysterious SallyOne was afraid of someone she knew. Fraser couldn't bear the thought of a puzzle piece like that slipping through her fingers.

13

SALLYONE453

Carol Fraser, the true crime YouTube influencer, sat in silence in the living room of her shared Edinburgh townhouse; her housemates at work in the city.

She stared at the printout from her livestream chat the evening before. Hundreds of lines; a back and fore between herself and the viewers.

But, right now, she was only interested in the commenter SallyOne453, who had started out with praise for the channel, then disappeared, leaving that enigmatic line hanging in the chat until it vanished at the top of her feed. What had SallyOne meant when she said, 'I could tell you some things about this killer'? And why would she leave the chat after putting that out there?

Carol picked up her phone, staring at the screen. Should she call DI McKenzie? Should she tell him this woman had made contact, even though she had no more information for him than that? The interaction felt significant, and yet the influencer was really no further forward regarding information about the killer who stalked the Greyfriars and Old Town areas.

Her heart beat faster as she contemplated the implications of the cryptic line. Had she stumbled upon someone who could provide a potential breakthrough in the investigation? Perhaps police could trace the elusive SallyOne.

Carol dialled McKenzie's number, her fingers trembling against the screen. As the number rang, she wondered if she was overreacting. After all, it was only one comment among many, and SallyOne453 could be nothing more than an attention-seeking troll.

But deep down, the influencer felt there was more to it. She had developed an intuition for her viewers over the years, connecting with them on a level beyond entertainment. SallyOne453's words resonated with her, stirring a sense of urgency that she simply couldn't ignore.

The DI's voice crackled through the phone. "Grant McKenzie..."

He must be outside, she thought. "Sir, this is Carol Fraser. I have something important to tell you regarding your investigation. I was live-streaming last night and received a comment from a user named SallyOne453. She claimed to know things about the killer you're looking for."

There was a brief pause on the other end before he responded. She could almost hear him contemplating her words. "Tell me everything, Carol. What exactly did this SallyOne453 say?"

She took a deep breath, her voice shaking. "She said, 'I could tell you some things about the killer.' And then she vanished from the chat without providing an explanation or anything further."

The DI's voice deepened. "It could be significant... But

we need more, like who SallyOne453 is and what she knows. Do you have contact information or traceable details from her account?"

Carol scrolled through the chat log. "I don't have specific contact information. I tried tracing her through her username and IP address, but I think she is using a VPN, so the IP is not a usable source."

"I see..." McKenzie thought about it. "I want you to forward me all the information you have on this Sally-One453. We'll have our tech team analyse it and see what they can uncover."

"No problem," Carol answered, jotting down his email address as he related it. She promised to send the details right away.

As she hung up, the influencer's mind raced with possibilities. SallyOne could be a witness who had seen something significant or heard a piece of information that could break the case wide open. Maybe SallyOne453 was connected to the killer in some way: a partner, accomplice, or relative. Perhaps she was inserting herself to find out what investigators had on him.

She hurriedly composed the email, detailing the brief interaction she had with SallyOne453 during the livestream, and attached screenshots of the chat log, hoping the details might be helpful to the police. This was her chance to make a difference, and perhaps contribute to solving the mystery that had gripped Edinburgh and the wider world.

As she hit send, watching the email disappear into the digital void, Carol felt a mixture of excitement and unease. She hoped it would help and not hinder the investigation, and that SallyOne had not simply been playing a cruel prank.

MCKENZIE PLACED his mobile back in his overcoat pocket.

He was back at the kirkyard and, after a brief chat with the uniformed officers on duty, he made his way to the steps where the body of James MacDonald had lain the week before.

The victim had been attacked from behind and, after SOCO had cleared away the snow, they found blood on the path above the steps where he had fallen after the assault. Bruising confirmed he hit them hard, sliding down several before ending up where the hapless Joan had found him.

Although the body had long since been taken away, McKenzie could still see it in his mind's eye as he cast his gaze around the kirkyard, trying to get into the head of the fiend wielding the knife, and the victim who had walked into the spider's web.

The perp had not taken the victim's camera. It remained with the body, still attached to the gimbal, leaving police with the eerie footage the unsuspecting creator had made as the killer stalked and murdered him, just like Margaret McLean.

Grant's eyes narrowed as he surveyed the kirkyard, his mind working through the twisted psychology of the murderer. He had seen his fair share of gruesome crime scenes, but something about this case gnawed at him, burrowing under his skin like a festering wound. That the perpetrator left behind the victims' equipment was no coincidence; it was a deliberate message; the footage, a macabre calling card. The killer wanted the world to witness the sound of atrocities first hand, so he could revel in the chaos and fear they caused.

The kirkyard gravestones stood tall and solemn, their dirty faces watching over secrets lying on and beneath the soil. He could almost feel the weight of history in the dank air.

As he walked among them, a sense of melancholy struck him, as if the spirits of the deceased were whispering to him, begging for justice to be served. The DI was certain the murders of Tam, Margaret, and James were not random acts of violence. There was a pattern; a method to the madness.

A light rain began falling from an overcast sky, adding to a spine-tingling ambience somehow befitting the kirkyard. His steps faltered as he passed a tall, wide gravestone with practically illegible etchings. As he made his way towards the weather-beaten stone, he weighed up possibilities. Could they have been ritual killings, driven by some deep-rooted belief? Or personal vendettas, scores being settled with each victim?

McKenzie knelt beside the tombstone, running gloved fingers along its moss-covered surface. He was almost certain this had been the place the killer waited with bated breath as his distracted prey approached.

Before leaving the kirkyard, the DI moved closer to the steps where James MacDonald had breathed his last. The bloodstains had faded, washed away by time and nature's cleansing hand, but he could picture it vividly. The violent clash between life and death had coloured his nightmares. His jaw tightened as he imagined MacDonald's last moments, and the fear and helplessness that must have consumed him. He could almost hear the crunch of snow beneath the murderer's boots as he walked away, no longer needing the stealth with which he approached.

But what drove this killer? Answering that question

might bring them closer to their psychopath. Perhaps Carol Fraser's SallyOne was the key. The DI telephoned the station, warning Graham and the team of Fraser's incoming email.

Dalgliesh promised to get right on it.

14

LIVESTREAMS

McKenzie was late back to the office and for a team meeting scheduled for two o'clock. It was twenty-past.

Susan, Graham, and Helen, already on their second coffee, had been considering giving up and going back to work.

"I'm sorry, I'm sorry." The DI stopped to catch his breath after running up two flights of stairs. "I didn't mean to keep you all waiting."

"Is everything okay?" Susan asked, getting up to fetch him a drink from the pot. She popped it in front of him as he removed his coat and took a seat. "You'll be needing this."

"Aye, thanks, Sue." He plopped his paperwork on the table. "I spent longer at the kirkyard than intended. I grabbed a sandwich on the way back so I wouldn't disrupt the meeting. It's been one of those mornings." He looked at Graham seated opposite. "Did you have any luck finding SallyOne's location?"

"I haven't got that far, yet." Dalgliesh scoured his notes. "But I can tell you she was a subscriber to the channels of all three of our murdered true crime sleuths. *And* she is a follower of Carol Fraser and Giles Douglas. Both of whom are still very much alive."

"And we want them to stay that way." Grant loosened his tie. "Has she commented on any of the other YouTubers' videos? Or livestreams?"

"That's what I was looking into before we came in here. And, as far as I have gone, there are one or two comments on each influencer's feed, praising their content. But she hadn't commented at all on Tam Fleming's work, bearing in mind he was the one who originally geo-profiled the sexual assaults around the Greyfriars and Old Town areas. Carol Fraser is the first one she contacted to say she has information. And, so far, she hasn't been back to elaborate."

"Has Carol tried contacting her?"

"She hasn't. And, although she has subscribers' emails, she is worried about making life difficult for SallyOne if, for instance, she is living with the perpetrator."

"But we can ask for Sally's contact details, right?"

"We can submit disclosure requests to YouTube, yes."

"It would need careful consideration. We don't want to make life difficult for SallyOne, either."

Grant leaned back in his chair, pondering the information Dalgliesh had shared. He took a sip of the coffee Susan had brought him, feeling the warmth spread through his body. He hadn't realised how cold he had gotten in the kirkyard. "Keep digging into SallyOne's online activity," Grant instructed Graham. "For now, we'll wait for her to contact Carol Fraser again. Keep the line of communication open with the YouTuber. Tell her we would like to know the minute SallyOne gets in contact."

"Aye, will do." The DC nodded.

"Has anything changed on our suspect list?"

Helen McAllister shook her head. "The six primary suspects haven't changed. We have Andy Scott, Margaret McLean's boyfriend who we met at her flat. A twenty-eight-year-old brick-layer from Glasgow, who didn't seem as distressed about her loss as we might expect. Then there are Martin Ross and Darren Paterson, volunteers at the kirk with the opportunity to commit the murders. Martin has anger issues, and was the second-to-last person leaving the kirk on the night James McDonald was murdered. And Darren Paterson is a retired teacher who looks after the grounds of the kirkyard and whose wife volunteers at the kirk. Then there is Tim Shaw, who organises the volunteers, and was the last person to leave the kirk on the night MacDonald was killed."

"Aye, and I had the distinct feeling he was tapping me for information about the crimes," the DI interjected.

"Right... And then, you thought maybe Gordon Caldwell? Barman and manager at the Greyfriars Bobby, who called in sick last minute on the day Margaret McLean was murdered. And finally, for the moment, Giles Douglas, another true crime influencer who takes exception to other YouTubers poaching or plagiarising content," McAllister finished.

"But we can't blame him for that. I think many YouTubers make similar complaints." Dalgliesh tapped his pen on the table.

"Agreed, but it provides another potential motive for the murders." McKenzie leaned forward on the desk, elbows bent; chin resting on his hands. "What about the shoe print we found in the kirkyard? Have we matched it to any of the suspects' shoes?"

Graham shook his head. "No, I'm afraid we haven't yet found a match, but even though it was only a partial print, forensics believe it was from a size eleven or twelve boot, and we have only examined shoes from potential suspects. It is possible the killer wore oversized boots and thick socks. We would need a warrant to search for the boots, and a solid suspect for that."

Grant agreed. "The print was a promising lead, but until we have a concrete suspect, it would be challenging to get a warrant. Focus on gathering more intel on each of the suspects," he suggested, sitting back in his chair. "Lets dig deeper into their backgrounds, alibis, and anything that might link them to the murders."

Helen nodded, grabbing a notepad and pen. "I'll start with Andy Scott. We know he didn't seem as distressed about Margaret McLean's death as we expected. Let's see if there's anything else suspicious about him."

Susan chimed in. "I'll look into Martin Ross and Darren Paterson. Find out whether there is a history of violence, or a connection to the influencers."

"Great," Grant nodded, "I'll focus on Tim Shaw and Gordon Caldwell. Leave no stone unturned. If there is anything else that could tie one of these people to the murders, we must find it and get enough information for a warrant to search for clothing and footwear linked to the deaths."

Tasks assigned, the team dispersed, each diving into their respective section of the inquiry. Grant retreated to his office, shutting the door behind him. He needed a moment to gather his thoughts and process the information they had so far.

As he sat at his desk, staring at the whiteboard covered with names and evidence, a nagging feeling tugged at the back of his mind. There was something they were missing, a piece that would unlock the raison d'être of this killer.

He drummed his fingers on the desk before continuing to watch Tam and Margaret's videos, looking for that key.

CAROL FRASER READIED herself for the latest livestream, checking her makeup and hair, and adjusting the lighting and camera for the best angle.

As the last five minutes ticked down to showtime, she wondered whether SallyOne would make an appearance. The influencer badly wanted to crack the case, imagining what a scoop it would be to give the police the information they needed for an arrest. The victims and their families would have justice, and her follower numbers were bound to swell as a result. And higher numbers meant more revenue from YouTube and maybe a home of her own, where she wouldn't have to label her food in the fridge, or come downstairs to the chaotic aftermath of some impromptu late-night party which her fellow housemates had thrown, and the smell of stale food and alcohol that always accompanied the mess.

But for now, Carol focussed on the livestream at hand. She took a deep breath, calming herself before hitting the "Go Live" button. Within seconds, her screen flooded with comments and questions from dedicated viewers.

"Hey, Carol! Love your content! Any update on the missing person case?"

"I heard there's a new lead in the Gimbal Killer case! Can you spill the tea, girl?"

Carol smiled at the excitement in her viewers' comments. She knew how desperate they were for the latest updates and the exclusive information she had a reputation for providing. She leaned closer to the camera.

"Good evening, all. Thanks for joining me tonight. As many of you know, we've been covering several cases in our beloved Edinburgh. I have one or two new pieces of information to share with you tonight, so we'll dig right into it." She paused. "I have something more on the Greyfriars murders, which we will cover later." Was SallyOne lurking? And, if she was, would that last bring her out of her shell and get her talking?

The comments section exploded with excitement and curiosity. Carol could barely keep up with the flurry of messages scrolling on her screen.

"Any idea who the killer might be?"

"Do you think it's someone from Edinburgh?"

"Tell us more..."

Taking a moment to compose herself, Carol cleared her throat and began, "Okay, I guess we can kick off with that case. According to my sources, there has been a fresh development in the police inquiry. They believe there is a connection between the Greyfriars murders and the killing of Tam Fleming, which they had previously believed was an attempted mugging in which the victim fought back. We had discussed on the livestreams how there could be a connection between Fleming's case and the Greyfriars attacks and now, finally, it is official. Police are also discussing the possibility of the sexual assaults being linked to the murders. So the kirkyard poltergeist may not be involved after all. But I think we all knew that, eh?" Carol paused for a minute, reading the chat. She joked, but there were indeed those who believed the wayward spirit of George 'Bloody' MacKenzie was responsible. Most of her viewers, however, were relieved the case was moving in the right direction.

'They are finally linking Tam's murder with the other killings... It's about time.'

'I always knew there was more to those sexual assaults. This is getting intense.'

'The police better catch this sicko soon. Edinburgh isn't safe anymore.'

Carol adjusted her camera, wanting to capture the excitement in her eyes for her audience. "Aye, you heard it right. The police are making progress in the investigation, connecting the dots between these cases. And here's what I've been thinking," she continued, relishing the role she played as the bearer of exclusive information and ideas. "Maybe the killer lurked among the subscribers on the victims' social media channels. I have some list-checking to do between now and my next podcast, but I think it is a real possibility. We know serial killers often enjoy taunting families or laughing at the public and police, but sometimes they also stalk or harass victims prior to attacking them."

SallyOne453: I think he watches them first.

CarolFr: What makes you say that, SallyOne?

Carol's heart beat fast. The woman she'd been waiting for was back.

SallyOne453: His routine, and the comings and goings.

CarolFr: Explain?

SallyOne did not come back.

CarolFr: SallyOne?

SallyOne453: I can't talk right now.

CarolFr: Can you DM me?

The influencer desperately wanted a direct message exchange, convinced SallyOne knew something. But the reluctant chatter did not get back.

Undeterred, Carol continued with her livestream, providing her viewers with the latest updates on the other cases she was covering, before delving into the psychology of serial killers and patterns of behaviour.

As she wrapped up the livestream, Carol felt frustrated but hopeful. SallyOne's sudden appearance in the chat only fuelled her curiosity further. She felt there was more to the interloper than met the eye, and she was determined to find out what SallyOne453 knew.

15

TROLL OR ENIGMA?

McKenzie scratched his head with the end of his pen, gazing out the window as he pondered the case.

DC Dalgliesh came in and perched on the end of his desk. Jacket off and sleeves rolled up, his look was intense as he related his findings to the DI. "I've been working with technicians to trace SallyOne453."

"What have you found?" Grant put his pen down.

"Her email on signup to Carol Fraser's channel was a randomly generated string of numbers instead of a name or nickname. Unfortunately, the app used can generate a new email as often as the user needs. Each time, it generates a new string of numbers. Providing the user verifies the email generated, they can make and change a new one at will. Sally, or her household, is also using a VPN, or Virtual Private Network." Dalgliesh pulled a face. "It's a tool which enables users to create a secure connection by masking their IP address, rerouting their internet traffic through different servers located all over the world. It encrypts their online activities, making it virtually impossible to trace their exact location or identity."

McKenzie leaned back in his chair, mulling over the information. "So, SallyOne is pretty good at covering her tracks," he remarked. "It seems to me she is going to great lengths to remain anonymous."

DC Dalgliesh nodded, his face serious. "Or a person she lives with has installed the extra security in order to hide their own communications."

"Do you think she shares her partner's email address?"

"We should consider that possibility. Some couples do."

Grant sighed, frustration clear in his voice. "This case is becoming more complicated by the minute. I'll speak with Carol Fraser again. Maybe she has heard something since we last spoke."

McKenzie grabbed his coat from the back of the chair and stood, ready to head out. He motioned for Graham to join him as he made his way towards the door. "Let's pay her another visit. Maybe she's heard something that can help us narrow our search."

They drove to Fraser's townhouse in silence, each detective lost in their own thoughts, the case weighing heavily on them.

Grant couldn't shake the feeling they were missing something crucial.

When they arrived at the influencer's doorstep, she greeted them with a weary smile, like she had stayed up late the night before. "You'd better come in," she said.

They followed her into the living room, where papers lay strewn across the floor.

"I've been cross-checking subscribers on the lists of the three murdered influencers, Tam Fleming, Margaret McLean, and James MacDonald. They had hundreds of thousands of subscribers each, so I have concentrated on any who made comments on their videos. I was looking specifically for names which appeared for all three of the victims." Carol pointed to her paperwork.

Grant and Graham exchanged glances. This was the work the DC had also been doing looking for SallyOne453.

"Well, I found a handful of subscribers who were present in all three streams," Carol explained, her fingers tapping the armrest of her chair. "But there was one name that stood out among the rest. TheWatcher246."

McKenzie leaned forward, his eyes narrowing with curiosity. "TheWatcher246? That's a suggestive name."

Carol nodded, her voice trembling with excitement. "Right, it is. And what's more unsettling is TheWatcher246 left cryptic messages in the comment sections of all three influencers' videos. They look innocent at first glance, but I believe each contained hidden references to their upcoming deaths."

Dalgliesh frowned. "References to their murders? Could you give us an example?"

She shuffled through the papers on the floor and pulled out a notepad. "Here," she said, sliding it across the coffee table. "Look at those..."

Grant lifted the pad, eyes scanning the messages in Carol's hurried scrawl.

"Look at this one," he said to Graham as he pointed to a comment on Tam Fleming's video. "The beauty of darkness is its ability to cloak that which would be seen. Unveiling the hidden shall reveal the truth."

Graham shrugged. "Sounds like nonsense to me, like someone wants to look all mysterious by writing gobbledegook."

The DI nodded. "You may be right, but the question is,

why? Why would they want to insert themselves and draw attention like that?"

"The internet is full of trolls."

"Aye, and this could be one of them... But the fact he followed all three influencers is interesting." Grant raised his eyes to Carol. "May I ask if he follows you?"

She nodded. "You can, and he doesn't. At least, as far as I can tell, he has never commented on any of my pre-recorded videos or livestreams."

"Have you looked at the dates in the comments?"

"I have, and the comments from The Watcher246 appeared in the week prior to the deaths of each of the victims."

The DI's brow furrowed. "Really? Could you give us copies of the comments with the dates and times the commenter left them? We'll do our own research, of course, but your work will give us a head start. I'm impressed." He grinned. "Who said you guys were armchair wannabes?"

She pulled a face at McKenzie's backhanded compliment. "Thank you, sir," she replied with a mock salute. "I'll gather the information you asked for and send it over as soon as I can."

As they left the influencer's home, the DI felt sure they were getting close. TheWatcher246 could be the missing link they needed. Was he the partner of SallyOne453? He broke the silence as they drove back to the station. "Darren and Joan Paterson keep coming to mind."

"Are you thinking they could be TheWatcher and Sally-One?" Dalgliesh asked.

"The husband looks after the kirkyard... What better

place to watch the victims from? Let's dig up what we can on TheWatcher246. Start by tracing his IP, if he isn't masking it."

Graham sighed. "I have a feeling he'll be hiding it just like SallyOne, but our technicians have worked miracles before. I'll keep on them."

CAROL SAT ENGROSSED in research on the bed with her laptop. As the sky grew dark, she switched on the bedside lamps but did not draw the curtains. She enjoyed being able to see the night sky as the world quietened outside. It gave her a different perspective, and an alternative ambience for thinking.

A notification popped up on her screen. It was a private message from SallyOne453.

SallyOne453: I'm sorry about the other night. I had to go.

The YouTuber sat up straight, fingers nervously tapping a response.

CarolFr: I was worried about you. Are you okay?

SallyOne453: Yeah, I'm fine.

CarolFr: What happened? Did someone come home?

SallyOne didn't answer.

CarolFr: Are you afraid of someone, Sally?

SallyOne453: Are you any closer to finding the killer?

CarolFr: I was hoping you had information for me? You implied so in one of my livestreams. Do you know something? Is there something you want to tell me? Is fear stopping you from talking?

SallyOne453: Maybe...

CarolFr: I'm here for you. We can get provide support, or

talk to people who can arrange a safe house for you. Somewhere you can stay without being in fear.

SallyOne453: You're right... I am afraid.

CarolFr: I thought so. Are you scared of someone who lives with you? Or of a friend? A relative? A co-worker? Do you suspect someone you know of being the Gimbal Killer?

CarolFr: Sally?

The sky turned black as Carol waited anxiously for Sally's response. The cursor, blinking on the screen, was a silent reminder of unanswered questions hanging in the digital air.

She was about to close her laptop when another message appeared.

SallyOne453: I can't say much, but I think I might know who the Gimbal Killer is.

CarolFr: I thought so... Please, tell me what you know. We can't let this monster continue roaming free around our Edinburgh.

SallyOne453: It's someone close to me, Carol. Someone I would never have suspected. He has been gaslighting me; making me doubt my sanity. I'm scared for my life.

The influencer paused. Was SallyOne a crank? She didn't think so. Her gut told her this was someone genuinely in fear for their safety.

CarolFr: We should involve the authorities, Sally. This is too dangerous for you, or us, to handle alone. Talk to me.

SallyOne453: He reads my messages. I'll have to delete this conversation.

CarolFr: Is he there, now?

SallyOne453: No.

CarolFr: In that case, can you tell me more?

SallyOne453: I'm scared he will find the stuff I've deleted. He's good with computers.

CarolFr: How about we meet in person. Would you do that? Somewhere he doesn't know, when you are sure he will be away for a while?

SallyOne453: I can't do that.

CarolFr: Why not, Sally?

CarolFr: Sally?

CarolFr: Sally, are you still there?

16

TO MEET OR NOT TO MEET?

McKenzie slipped through the wrought-iron gate of the old kirkyard, his gaze drawn to the solitary figure of Darren Paterson. The morning mist, like a mysterious blanket, clung to the weathered tombstones, whirling against the Flodden Wall, and muffling the sounds of the waking city.

Paterson was hunched over, clearing debris from what had been the McLean crime scene.

The DI approached in silence as he observed Paterson's meticulous care with the groundwork in the damp kirkyard. The volunteer's movements were rhythmic and reverent as his rake erased all signs of the horror which unfolded only weeks before.

The detective's eyes narrowed, studying the man's every gesture for some telltale flicker of guilt or remorse. But Paterson's face remained impassive, focused solely on his task. He appeared not to notice the advancing detective.

In the soft whisper of leaves rustling in the breeze, Margaret McLean's image came unbidden to Grant's mind. Propped against the cold grey tombstone, her lifeless eyes stared into his soul, haunting him with their silent plea. 'Find him,' they said.

He felt a tightening in his chest, the weight of responsibility never more pressing. He closed his eyes, dispelling the vision, yet her presence lingered in the blackness of his closed lids. "Margaret," he answered in thought. "I'm trying."

A creak came from the doors of the kirk, and the DI pulled back, stepping behind one of the taller gravestones.

Joan Paterson emerged, her steps tentative as she approached her husband.

Darren straightened, resting a hand on the small of his back as he turned to greet her.

McKenzie strained to listen.

"We need to talk," Joan's voice carried on the breeze.

"I'm working," her husband responded, leaning his rake against the nearest headstone and wiping his hands on his trousers. "Can it wait?"

Grant watched, noting the taut line of Joan's shoulders, and the way her hands clasped and unclasped in front of her. She shook her head, her words muffled but tone insistent as she took a step closer to Darren. "Something's not right. This isn't just about that poor woman..." Her voice trailed off, eyes darting around the kirkyard as though searching for an eavesdropping spirit among the graves.

Darren waved a large hand at her. "Wheesht, it's all in your head, woman."

Joan paced next to him.

Paterson said something the DI couldn't quite grasp and reached out to grab his wife.

The DI held his breath, but checked an urge to intervene, preferring instead to know the man's intention.

Mrs Paterson pulled her hands away from her husband,

wrapping her arms around herself. "I hope you're right," she murmured before turning back towards the church, her figure retreating into the sanctuary's shadow.

As the door closed behind her, McKenzie seized the moment. He stepped forward, shoes crunching over gravel, closing the distance between himself and the volunteer.

"Morning, Darren," the DI announced, causing the groundskeeper to jump, the rake clattering against the stone.

"Jings! You nearly gave me a heart attack."

"Sorry about that," McKenzie apologised, though his sharp eyes darted over the man's startled face. "Are you and your wife okay? I couldn't help but notice your discussion."

"Och, it was nothing important... family matters, you know?" Paterson retrieved his rake, leaning on it in attempted nonchalance that didn't quite ring true.

"I see..." Grant nodded, his gaze holding Paterson's. "You've done a good job of tidying up."

"Thanks" Darren looked uncomfortable, running a hand through greying hair. He stood at full height and was a good couple of inches taller than the DI.

Mckenzie was not intimidated. "How have things been in the kirkyard? Have you noticed anything suspicious?"

"No."

"Anyone hanging around more than usual?"

Paterson shook his head. "No."

"Right, I'll let you carry on." Grant could tell Paterson had no wish to speak to him. His reluctance didn't make him guilty, but it got the DI's attention. What was the man hiding?

∿

THE PERSISTENT HUM of her laptop accompanied a rhythmic tapping as Carol's fingers roamed her keyboard. She glanced at the screen; her livestream chat steadily scrolling with comments from followers. The glow from her monitor and a soft desk lamp created an intimate and eerie ambience for the mystery she dissected piece by piece with her audience. That night, her show had garnered more interest than usual.

"Okay, folks," she said, tiredness leaking through the husky voice streaming to viewers, "let's circle back to the alibi provided by our suspect in the last episode."

The livestream was almost done, and the influencer was about to cover endpoints when her eyes caught a familiar name in the chat window and her heart jumped. The last time Sally-One453 appeared, her cryptic messages hinted at knowing more about the Gimbal Killer than was public knowledge.

CarolFr: SallyOne453, welcome back.

She kept her tone neutral, not wishing to scare away the person she had been waiting for, and sipped lukewarm coffee, her gaze locked on the chat.

SallyOne453: Carol, I need to tell you something important.

CarolFr: Great, I can't wait to hear what you have.

The cursor blinked in the chat box, everyone waiting for the response from SallyOne.

The influencer took a deep breath. Was SallyOne453 seeking attention, or did she have genuine information that would benefit the case?

CarolFr: Hey, SallyOne453?

Anxiety knotted her stomach.

CarolFr: SallyOne453, DM me, please?

She hit enter and waited, eyes darting between the chat and the private message notification icon. The rest of the chat continued on with theories and questions. But Carol's focus was on one name, waiting for the crucial interaction that might tip the scales on the investigation.

Seconds felt like hours.

Finally, the notification bell lit up; a private message from SallyOne453. The influencer exhaled, steadying herself for whatever was about to come through the wires, knowing full well it could change everything.

She clicked on the message, fingers poised above the keyboard like a pianist about to start a concerto.

SallyOne453: I'm sorry I didn't get back to you sooner.

CarolFr: No problem... Last time, you implied you knew something important?

SallyOne453: Maybe, but it's complicated. There was a pause before the next message popped up. "I'm worried."

CarolFr: Understandable. But I can help you if you let me. We just need to be careful.

The YouTuber's mind worked overtime as thought how best to tease out the information she craved.

CarolFr: Can we meet?

Carol grimaced. The question might appear too needy. Her sense of urgency bleeding through the texts.

SallyOne453: Danger is everywhere. It should be a public space.

CarolFr: Of course... We should take this one step at a time. Whatever you feel comfortable with.

SallyOne453: I doubt it will feel comfortable wherever we go.

CarolFr: I know. We will both be nervous, but you can trust me.

SallyOne453: Okay yes, I'll do it.

CarolFr: Good. Do you have a place in mind?

Carol reminded herself to breathe. This was tentative progress.

SallyOne453: Let me think for a moment.

CarolFr: No problem.

She sat back in her chair, mind ticking over the potential consequences of their meeting. The flickering cursor on the screen was a silent metronome counting down the seconds as she waited for SallyOne to suggest a place and time.

SallyOne453: How about Princes Street Gardens? This Thursday at three in the afternoon?

CarolFr: Princes Street Gardens it is.

The familiarity of the location offered a thin slice of comfort to the influencer. She had always found solace among the lush greenery in that park. A place where the bustle of daily life slipped away. It was an excellent suggestion by SallyOne.

SallyOne4532: See you there.

Sally punctuated the message with a simple smiley face emoji that seemed out of place, given the hesitancy of her earlier exchange.

As the chat window fell silent, Carol worried their intended rendezvous might endanger SallyOne. What if the person she feared read her messages? The stillness as she closed her computer, usually peaceful and relaxing, felt ominous. Each creak and whisper of the old townhouse amplified that unease.

"I should tell them..." she muttered to herself, picturing the faces of McKenzie and his team. She had promised to let them know if SallyOne got in touch again. And yet, to tell them would be to betray Sally's trust, wouldn't it? And SallyOne might be an online troll weaving tales for attention. Carol could almost hear the chiding voices of the MIT, cautioning her about leading them on wild goose chases and wasting police time.

With a sigh, she paced to the window, the decision gnawing at her. To involve police prematurely might scare off SallyOne or put them both in danger if the woman's identity was exposed. Yet, to go to the park without police knowledge was to walk blindly into the unknown, and without help if anything went wrong. "Damned if I do, damned if I don't," she whispered, gazing into the night.

Silhouetted trees swayed in the breeze, like the stoic sentinels that would guard the secrets being passed in Princes Street Gardens. There, under the watchful eye of nature, Carol hoped to finally learn the truth.

17

A NEW LEAD?

From the other end of the aisle, between the sauces and canned soups, he watched her.

Carol Fraser moved between fellow shoppers with elegance, belying the mundane chore at hand. She reached for a box of high-fibre cereal, her slender fingers grazing over the cardboard as she inspected the ingredients and calories.

"Excuse me," another woman attempted to squeeze past Carol's trolley.

"Oh, I'm sorry." Carol offered a smile that didn't reach her eyes, but sufficed for the brief interaction. Her distraction prevented her from offering more than that. Still, she moved aside with grace.

Her watcher noted how effortlessly she navigated the social niceties, even while not paying attention. He wondered if it would be the same when she unwittingly walked towards her final breath.

"Choosing the healthy option, eh?" A middle-aged male member of the shop staff peered into Carol's basket.

She clearly knew him. "Aye, healthier than last week." She

chuckled. "I decided I've to make an effort. I cannae survive on pizza and ready meals, no matter how busy I am."

The watcher felt a pang of jealousy. It travelled up his back and over his scalp. Enough already, he thought, get on with your work, man.

"Well, you're headed in the right direction." The assistant gave the young woman a wink.

"I'm trying..." Carol replied, her voice light, but tinged with weariness at the effort of maintaining small talk. It gave the watcher some satisfaction.

"Good for you, lassie. We've got to look after ourselves. Nobody will do it for us, eh?" The man patted her on the shoulder before moving on.

The watcher lingered a moment, watching her turn down the next aisle, the curve of her waist calling like a siren song. He took in the rhythm of her gait, and the occasional flip of her straw-blonde hair. It ignited something dark within him. As she perused the labels on various jars of pasta sauce, her brow furrowed in concentration, he could almost taste the salt of her skin, feel the flutter of a terrified pulse under his fingertips.

The fluorescent lighting of the supermarket cast a sterile glow on everything it touched, yet Carol seemed to move in softer light, a warmth in contrast to the cold shine reflecting off the linoleum-tiled floor. Her petite frame spoke of vulnerability. He clenched his hands in anticipation.

Carol laughed at something the cashier said while ringing up her groceries. The watcher felt desire tighten his throat—a choking cocktail of lust and a thirst for dominance. Fixated on her every move, he was certain she would make the perfect prey. But not here, amidst the beeps of scanners and the banal chatter of shoppers. He could wait for the dance of predator and prey to reach its inevitable conclusion.

Oblivious, Carol pushed her shopping cart through the auto-

matic doors. The cool evening breeze cut across the supermarket's
threshold, swirling blossom around her feet. The car park was
alive with the sound of trolleys, engines starting up, and cars
manoeuvring out and around the spaces with the squelch of tyres
on tarmac.

As she navigated towards her vehicle, keys jangling in her
hand, the young woman was once more unaware of the eyes that
followed.

DC HELEN MCALLISTER LEANED FORWARD, eyes flicking across the computer screen as she deep dived into the digital lives of the Giles Douglas and Carol Fraser. The soft whirr of computers and the occasional chirp from the police radio provided the soundtrack, along with low chatter from the rest of the Major Investigation Team. For Helen, the world had shrunk to the virtual exchanges she monitored, and it had her absorbed.

"Found anything?" McKenzie came over to hover close, but without peering over the DC's shoulder, conscious of respecting her personal space.

"Potentially..." Helen replied without taking her eyes off the screen. She clicked through several pages, her fingers deftly navigating the keyboard. "Carol has reconnected with SallyOne."

"She has?" The DI grabbed a chair to sit down next to McAllister.

"Don't get too excited." Helen pulled a face, minimising one window to pull up another. "They switched to direct messaging as their primary means of communication. We would need help, and special permissions to access those. And you know what big tech is like. They don't give up user data without a fight." She turned her monitor so he could see the transcript of Carol and Sally's initial exchange.

Graham and Susan came over to join them, as Helen scrolled through the few messages she had access to, highlighting key points. "I think they might meet up. The problem is, without accessing the direct messages, we don't know where."

"Let's get the permission requests in as soon as possible." The DI folded his arms. "They may both be in grave danger. That is a reasonable basis on which to request access. But good work, Helen, stay with it. This feels like progress."

"There's something else."

"Go on..." Grant leaned in.

"Look at this," she said, tapping a highlighted section of text with her finger. "There was a terse exchange between Giles and Carol the other day." She pointed to a comment on one of Fraser's videos. It read, 'Your creativity seems to have taken an uncanny leap since you laid eyes on my recent work, Carol.'

McKenzie frowned. "He thinks she's stealing his ideas."

"Looks like it." Helen sat back in her chair. "And there, you see her response."

'I don't need to stoop to theft, Giles. Maybe if you spent more energy on content and less on your plagiarism conspiracy theories, you'd see that. And this isn't the place to get into facile discussions. We do our own research on this channel, and do not need to take ideas from you or anyone else.'

"Hardly the cosy camaraderie of fellow influencers," quipped DS Robertson, her lips pursed as she studied the transcript over Helen's shoulder.

"Exactly," the DC agreed. "It's controlled, but it's there— the rivalry, and bitterness. And this isn't the first time I've seen Douglas lash out when he feels his ideas are being poached."

The DI's brow furrowed. "He was obviously annoyed with fellow creators the last time we saw him. I am not entirely surprised at this exchange, but I am concerned about it. Has Douglas had spats with others? In particular, with any of those who were murdered?"

"I found similar jibes at other influencers, including those who wound up dead." Helen's reply hung in the room, like a storm cloud waiting to burst.

"There are few coincidences in our line of work," McKenzie pursed his lips. "I think we should bring Mr Douglas in for another chat, see if he's as creative in his explanations as he claims to be in his work."

"Agreed." Helen gathered sheets of paper into a neat stack. "These are the printouts of his altercations with others. We can confront him with each one and see what he has to say. He can hardly deny them if we put the evidence in front of him. Incidentally, I haven't found a single compliment from him to other creatives. His conversations with them have only involved intellectual theft, and sometimes right before things went south for them." Helen's words held an undercurrent of excitement at the possibility of having made a breakthrough.

"Did he have replies from any of the victims?" asked DC Dalgliesh, his broad frame casting a shadow over the screen.

"Nothing in depth," Helen replied. "They mostly responded with denials or attempts to brush him off. The date and timestamps line up reasonably closely with their murders, and certainly within two to three weeks for each."

"Maybe our guy felt so threatened by other influencers he silenced them permanently," murmured Robertson, her face sombre.

"But that doesn't take into consideration the sexual assaults which we think were linked." McKenzie frowned.

"But who says they have to be related. Maybe the murderer is not the person committing the assaults. We assumed right out of the gate that it must be, but maybe the only link is the sleuths' investigations of the assaults, and not the attacks themselves."

"You could be right, Helen." McKenzie nodded. "I admit I could be wrong about the assaults being connected," he agreed.

"Let me see those again," Dalgliesh reached for the printouts from Helen. The papers rustled as he spread them out on the table.

"Notice the language," Helen tapped a finger on the pages. "Douglas is meticulous and calculated. He stops short of outright threats, but there's an undercurrent..."

"Of menace." Susan finished the sentence, her gaze lifting to meet her colleague's. "His words are enough to unsettle the target, but not enough to break the law."

"Right..." Helen nodded, satisfied they were on the same page.

"Sounds like we've got a new prime suspect." Dalgliesh's quiet words settled on each member of the team. They exchanged looks of grim agreement. Giles Douglas had moved to the top of their list.

"Dig deeper into Douglas's history; see if he has challenged anyone else and, if he has, did anything physical occur afterwards?" McKenzie stood, pushing his hands deep into his trouser pockets. "And let's get him in for questioning."

18

DANGER LURKS

Cold air nipped her face, blushing her cheeks. Although spring was well underway, winter's claws scraped the land as the new season dragged it away by the ankles. Carol had with her a camera bag and tripod, hoping Sally would agree to the meeting being filmed for use at some future time, once they had neutralised any threat.

Princes Street Gardens was beautiful at this time of year. The historic green space, nestled in the heart of Edinburgh, held a rich tapestry of emerging life. Crocuses and daffodils dotted the grass with bursts of colour, while newly budded leaves unfurled in the late afternoon sun.

The garden unfolded through a canopy of ethereal cherry blossom which cast dappled shadows on the pathway below.

Rhododendrons burst forth in vibrant hues, beside beds of tulips nodding gently in the breeze. Manicured lawns provided a lush carpet of green, inviting visitors to relax and bask in their tranquil spaces.

To the East, the iconic Scott Monument loomed, its

Gothic spire reaching toward the heavens; intricate detailing highlighted against a clear, azure sky. To the West, Edinburgh Castle lay atop Castle Rock, its ancient stones adding an age-old majesty to the park's backdrop, while the gently babbling Water of Leith gave a sense of solace in harmony with rustling leaves overhead. Benches strategically placed along the riverbank offered a perfect vantage point for watching the world go by. But Carol wasn't here to while away time. She was here to meet SallyOne, as they had agreed. It was for this reason, her heart beat faster as she pulled her coat tight around her; the chill wasn't because of the breeze sweeping across the park's expanse, but trepidation at her meeting with the enigmatic woman.

"Are you Sally?" she asked a woman passing by with her dog.

A polite shake of the head confirmed she was not.

"Excuse me, have you seen a woman waiting? Perhaps looking around for someone?" she asked an elderly couple perched on a nearby bench.

"No, sorry," they answered. "What does she look like?"

Carol blanched, unable to answer their question. She shrugged and moved on.

Deeper into the garden, she paused, feeling eyes on her. Glancing over her shoulder, she saw only a jogger and a young couple out for a leisurely stroll.

"Keep it together, Carol. You're paranoid because of everything that's happened," she muttered to herself.

UNSEEN, a shadow detached itself from the knot of trees to her left. It moved with purpose, keeping pace with the desperately searching woman. The stalker was patient, his steps muffled by soft earth. He knew the layout of the gardens as intimately as his own twisted thoughts, slipping between scots pines and silver birches with practiced ease.

"Are you here, SallyOne?" Carol muttered, eyes scouring the garden paths, holding hope and frustration in equal measure. "Please don't tell me you changed your mind..."

The watcher bided his time. The young woman's vulnerability was palpable, and the isolation he'd been waiting for, nearly complete. Finally, the last of the garden's visitors thinned to nothing. His prey was alone.

"Come on..." Carol's plea dissipated in the open air, her breath forming small clouds in front of her face. She rubbed her arms for warmth, unaware of the stalker closing in.

A shiver ran down her spine, a prescient whisper of danger lurking. Why had Sally asked to meet her here? Worried eyes scanned the blossoming cherry trees and grand old elms, silent sentinels watching over the garden. She swallowed hard, increasingly aware of how exposed she now was. She wished she had met her mum for coffee, the original plan before SallyOne joined her livestream only a few nights before.

McKenzie manoeuvred the unmarked police vehicle through the snarl of Leith's midday traffic, his eyes rarely leaving the road, save for the occasional sidelong glance at Dalgliesh. "What do you think, Graham? Could Douglas be our man? He doesn't strike me as someone who could deal with that much chaos in his life. Do you remember how structured and controlled everything was in his place?"

"He strikes me as an obsessive. And, I agree, I doubt it would sit comfortably with him, dealing with mess and the aftermath of murder." Dalgliesh pressed his lips together. "Though I think he would find it hard to let go of perceived wrongs without retaliating. And if he's as clever as we believe, he would likely plan any such attack meticulously."

"We need to find him, and fast." Grant's fingers tightened around the wheel.

The outside world transitioned from the industrial hues of Leith to the historic grandeur of Edinburgh's Old Town, where cobbled streets and looming tenements evoked an earlier age. Overcast skies rendering the ancient buildings a foreboding air, as though nature herself sensed the detectives' concern.

"Right, we're here." McKenzie pulled up to the old building which housed Giles Douglas's flat.

They stepped out into the chill, pulling their coats tight and collars up against the biting wind that funnelled down the narrow street; eyes blinking against the stinging street dust.

"Looks dark in there, and quiet," Dalgliesh observed, his gaze sweeping up the structure before landing on the secured entrance. "Too quiet?"

"Only one way to find out." McKenzie led the way, striding up the staircase to the door of Douglas's loft apartment and buzzing the intercom.

The only answer was static, followed by silence. Grant pressed the button again, holding it longer this time, his jaw tightening when the result was the same. Giles Douglas was out.

19

THE ABANDONED TRIPOD

They arrived at Carol's shared Georgian townhouse in late afternoon, as the sun sank lower in the sky. The tall sash windows were closed, and the place lay silent.

Dalgliesh's eyes scanned the upper floors, expecting to glimpse movement behind the heavy drapes. None was forthcoming.

McKenzie grabbed his overcoat from the back seat of the car, as the chill wind had not abated. "Let's hope Ms Fraser can shed some light on Giles Douglas."

They approached the glossed black door, with its elegant brass knocker, which the DC was about to rap until he spotted a slip of paper attached with sticky tape. He plucked it free.

He handed it to the DI. "She's not here."

"It's a message to her mother." Grant read aloud, "'Mum, I am sorry I cannot do coffee this afternoon. Had to go out. I am filming in Princes Street Gardens. Will be back in around five o'clock. Love you, Carol.'"

"Filming?" Dalgliesh raised an eyebrow. "And she cancelled a coffee date with her mum?"

McKenzie frowned. "Why would she change her plans to make a video at short notice?" He looked at Graham. "Something's up."

"Do you think she could be meeting SallyOne?" Graham placed the note back on the door.

"I do, and I think we need to get there yesterday."

THEY SPED TO THE GARDENS, parking as close as they were able before running on foot to the entrance gates.

"Keep focused. We have to find her." The DI scanned their surroundings. Manicured lawns sprawling ahead of them were empty save for a woman walking a cocker spaniel. Shadows from the trees lengthened as the sun dipped lower in the sky.

"Over there," Dalgliesh pointed toward a grove of cherry blossoms, their petals fluttering to the ground. A camera tripod stood abandoned, one leg collapsed, the apparatus tilted at an unnatural angle.

"Damn it." McKenzie's pace quickened. "That's not a good sign."

"It's probably Fraser's, eh?" Graham looked over the tripod, his voice trailing off as he bent to pick up a small yellow scarf lying at the base. He held it up, its fabric shimmering in the late afternoon sun. "This could be hers."

"Let's fan out," The DI ordered, his instruction terse. "Call this in. We'll need backup for a search. I want eyes on every corner of these gardens."

"Got it." Dalgliesh grabbed his radio to relay their location and the situation to control as he and McKenzie moved deeper into the gardens.

McKenzie passed under the boughs of blossoming trees, all of his senses alert. "Stay sharp," he reminded the DC. "We don't know what we might face here."

A GLOVED HAND clamped over her mouth from behind; an arm, solid and unyielding, wrapped around her torso, lifting her off her feet. Panic surged through bulging veins, as her heart pounded a frantic rhythm between her ribs. Carol's muffled screams barely carried past the hand on her face.

"Quiet," a voice hissed in her ear, low and menacing. "Not another sound, or it'll be the last one you make."

The attacker dragged her toward a secluded copse shaded by dense foliage. Carol's mind raced, survival instincts screaming for her to fight and flee, but a fear-addled mind and body would not respond. She struggled, but was not strong enough to break free.

"Stop squirming," the attacker growled, his sweaty breath hot on her face.

They were in a secluded part of the garden, birdsong eerily absent, the creatures having scattered when the attack started. Carol could hear soft strains of the city beyond the thick curtain of greenery. A shoe left behind on the gravel path was the only sign of resistance as the attacker and victim disappeared from view.

"Please," she pleaded, her voice barely audible. "You don't have to do this." She would have continued begging, but her attacker had stilled, head stiff and alert, eyes up. He was listening.

She prayed it was someone approaching along the path.

"Help," she squealed. "Help-" He struck her across the face before clamping his hand once more over her mouth.

"DID YOU HEAR THAT?" Grant halted, swivelling his head this way and that, holding up a hand for Graham to listen. "Over there," he whispered, pointing to an area covered by thick bushes.

The DC nodded, eyes scouring the foliage.

They moved in tandem, feet silent on the grass.

"He's close, I know it," McKenzie said, his voice low as he navigated the rhododendrons.

Without warning, the bushes parted, and the attacker emerged, hauling Carol by her arm. The young woman's mouth lay open in terror; eyes wide and pleading. In the assailant's other hand, the unmistakable glint of a blade, sharp and menacing.

"Woah!" McKenzie's voice was strained as he held his hands up in fear for the danger Fraser was in, his focus narrowing on the knife and the threat it posed.

"Tim Shaw..." Dalgliesh spat the words, his disgust clear. He clenched his fists, surveying the dishevelled male holding the girl.

"Stay calm," Grant advised in a low voice, aiming to soothe both Carol and her captor. "We can resolve this." His eyes never left the blade, watching it as though it were a serpent poised to strike. He approached slowly.

"Back off!" Shaw glared at them, his command cutting through the tense air like a razor. He stood defiant, face distorted by a snarl, his stance wide and unyielding as he clutched Carol's arm tighter, the knife in his other hand held threateningly close to her throat.

Grant froze mid-step, eyes narrowing. The man in front had portrayed himself as a pillar of the community, always ready with a smile and a helping hand at Greyfriars Kirk. As the DI's heart thumped in his chest, it was impossible to reconcile this mud-stained, dishevelled version with the smartly dressed, easygoing man who organised charity events and guided tours through the historic aisles of the kirk.

"Stay back!" The attacker delivered the words in a guttural roar, his knuckles whitening as he pressed the blade perilously close to the woman's neck. The look in his eyes, wild, primal, and desperate.

McKenzie, still with palms facing Shaw, held his breath. Every muscle and sinew wound tight. He emitted a calm he was far from feeling. "Tim... listen to me," he began, his tone steady and deliberate. "You don't want to do this. You don't want to hurt Carol. Think about the people at Greyfriars, and how they look up to you." He took a cautious step forward, risking a closeness that could defuse or detonate the situation.

"Don't talk!" Shaw barked, his eyes darting back and forth as he tried to figure a way out of the situation.

Dalgliesh eased beside the DI. "Let's talk about this, Tim. Whatever's going on, we can help, but not if you hurt her."

"I don't want your help," Shaw spat the words, but with a perceptible shake in the hand which held the knife.

The DI took another step forward.

20

THE GIMBAL KILLER

McKenzie's jaw clenched, his eyes on Shaw's face. He could feel the tension radiating from Dalgliesh beside him.

"Tim," The DI kept his voice low. "Let's talk about this. Tell us what you need and let the girl go. We can't let you leave, and holding her will only make things harder for you in the long run."

The man's wild eyes flicked towards Grant, then to Graham, calculating, distrustful. He lifted the knife higher under the woman's chin in agitation.

Wide-eyed, Carol's breath came in sharp, erratic bursts above the weapon's edge.

"Easy there," Graham said, his tone equally composed. "We're all here to help. No one needs to get hurt, okay?"

BEHIND THEM, the air began vibrating with the thud of boots as an armed response unit moved into position, accompanied by the distant bark of police dogs, and the rhythmic thud-thud-thud of helicopter blades slicing through the early evening air. The sounds were reassuring for Carol and the detectives, a reminder of strength and support, but they served as an unspoken ultimatum to Shaw.

Carol whimpered, a small sound that tightened Grant's chest. As a negotiator, he knew the importance of empathy, of forging a human connection, even with someone as volatile as Shaw. He took a slow step forward, hands open and visible.

"Lay down your weapon, Tim. This lady has done you no wrong. You don't really want to hurt her, do you?" Mckenzie delivered every word in a tone intended to diffuse rather than ignite.

"Stay back!" Shaw's voice cracked like a whip as he pressed the knife against Carol's skin, eliciting another gasp from her.

"Nobody's coming any closer," Grant assured, halting his advance. "Just talk to us, Tim. What do you need?"

The persistent churn of the helicopter overhead melded with a distant canine symphony, a discordant orchestra accompanying the high-stakes drama playing out in Princes Street Gardens. Grant and Graham exchanged glances, knowing they had to keep the attacker talking, engaged, and away from the brink. The situation could deteriorate at any moment.

BEYOND the newly constructed police cordon, a crowd materialised like flies to a corpse. Curiosity craned their necks as they tried to get a glimpse of the drama unfolding in the gardens. One or two, likely reporters, ducked under the police tape.

McKenzie's jaw clenched. Bystanders complicated things and the margin for error was already razor thin. "Keep them back," he muttered to Dalgliesh, who nodded, brow furrowed as he relayed the command through his radio.

Shaw's eyes darted from the encroaching armed unit to the detectives four feet away. Sweat glistened on his brow as he shifted weight from one foot to the other, the knife at Carol's throat glinting ominously with every twitch of his hand.

"Look at me, Tim," Grant's voice cut through the tension, firm but calm. "Don't worry about other people... This is between us."

"Wheesht!" Shaw shouted, ragged; breathless. His gaze flickered to the circling helicopter as he began backing up, pulling the influencer with him. He was searching for a gap, an escape route where none existed.

"Tim," the DI tried again, adopting the tone he'd used countless times to de-escalate a standoff, "there's no way out through there. But there is a way out through me. Let's sort this."

Dalgliesh remained silent as he watched Shaw like a predator tracking prey, waiting for a slip, a falter, any sign that could be used to their advantage; every muscle ready to pounce should the opportunity present itself.

McKENZIE'S FINGERS TWITCHED, aching for action as he locked eyes with Carol's attacker. The man's knuckles were white against the knife handle, like the pallor of the captive's petrified face. Her breaths came in gasps, audible even with the incessant thrumming of the helicopter above.

$\sim$

"LET THE GIRL GO," Grant ordered, keeping his voice steady despite the adrenaline coursing through his veins. "Put the knife down and let her loose."

They kept pace with Shaw as he backed up, their shoes barely whispering on the grass. Every step calculated, every breath controlled. Their gaze not wavering from Shaw's quivering hand, the hand that held a life in balance.

The helicopter was now overhead; the wind from its blades almost knocking them over.

McKenzie looked up in irritation.

In a flash of chaotic movement, Shaw pushed Carol aside with such force she stumbled to the ground.

"Run!" The DI bellowed to her, even as he surged forward with Graham close on his heels.

Shaw bolted, instinct overtaking reason, cries tearing from his throat.

The canines, trained for exactly this scenario, launched after him with a ferocity that terrified their target. Barks, echoing around the park, joined Shaw's wails of pain and fright as they caught up, latching onto a flailing arm and leg.

They heard the fabric of Shaw's trousers tear in the dogs' jaws as he tried to escape. But he was no match, and they dragged him down, their bodies taut as they pinned the struggling Shaw on the ground.

Armed officers ran to him, along with Dalgliesh and McKenzie.

Air, previously thick with tension and fear, held only the ragged breathing of the captive and the panting of the dogs, as their handlers pulled them away.

"Stay down," McKenzie commanded, his voice like steel, as he closed the distance.

"Clear!" one of the armed officers called, confirming he had secured Shaw's wrists in cuffs behind his back, neutralising the threat.

GRANT KNELT BESIDE CAROL, who lay crumpled on the ground, her breaths shallow and ragged.

Her wide eyes met his, a storm of emotions swirling in their depths. Fear, relief, and shock fought for dominance as tears spilled over.

"You're safe now..." Grant reassured her, his tone more gentle that the one he used with Shaw. "It's over."

Graham pulled off his jacket and draped it over the trembling woman, a barrier between her and the evening chill while paramedics made their way over to assess her.

"You won't be needing any excitement for a while after this, eh?" Grant teased, the accent of his native Edinburgh wrapping around her like a blanket. "We'll leave you with these guys for now and take a statement from you when you are ready."

Carol nodded, her gaze on the handcuffed Shaw being led away by armed men. She drew a shuddering breath, straightening her clothing and regaining control after the harrowing ordeal. "Thank you," she whispered.

"Nothing to thank us for," Grant replied as he stood up, allowing her to be stretchered towards a waiting ambulance. "Get some rest."

As sirens wailed in the distance, the dispersing crowd murmured like the Leith Waters winding through the park.

The two detectives left the gardens to find their vehicle.

21

CASE CRACKED

The chill in the dank Edinburgh air felt fitting as McKenzie crossed the threshold of Greyfriars Kirkyard. To visitors and tourists, the ancient stones represented dark secrets of the city's past, but for McKenzie, they murmured of more recent atrocities. He paused, his gaze falling upon the temporary memorials for Margaret McLean and James MacDonald, standing out like wounds against the weathered backdrop. Flowers, spent candles, and messages surrounded them; poignant evidence of a community's grief. The plight of the victims weighed heavily on his mind. But those victims would soon have justice; their killer was now inside a prison where he belonged.

As the DI wended his way through the labyrinth of tombstones, he spotted Darren Paterson hunched over a neglected grave, scraping away at stubborn moss which clung to a barely discernible script. The volunteer gardener's hands were stained green and brown. McKenzie watched him with a pang of guilt at having suspected him of the murders.

"Mr Paterson?" Grant paused, not wanting to startle the concentrating man.

Paterson looked up, blinking in the sunlight, his expression one of surprise. "DI McKenzie..." he nodded the greeting as he straightened, brushing debris from his knees.

"You're doing a great job." The DI stepped closer, hands buried deep in the pockets of his coat.

"I try." Darren looked back at the stone. "The dead deserve our care, don't you think?"

McKenzie nodded, the faces of McLean and MacDonald once again in his mind's eye. "They do, indeed." He cleared his throat before continuing. "I wanted to see how you were doing, and..." He hesitated, searching for the right words, "to apologise for being harsh on you. The city and this community need people like you. Dedicating your spare time freely for others."

Darren's shoulders, which had tensed in anticipation of judgment, relaxed at the DI's warm sincerity. "It's okay. I understood your position. These are strange times we find ourselves in. The world has gone a wee bit crazy. Suspicion is the heavy cloak all of us wear these days. But, in your job, you can never take it off."

"I'm grateful for your understanding. The last thing we want is to alienate stalwarts of the community." McKenzie extended a hand, which Darren accepted, their gentleman's shake bridging the gap that doubt and suspicion had carved.

"Take care of yourself, Mr Paterson. And thank you, for all you do here," Grant's eyes swept over the kirkyard—a final salute to the living soul tending to resting spirits.

"Aye, will do. You too..." The volunteer turned back to his task. "Keep fighting the good fight."

The DI left the kirkyard behind, feeling more at peace as his echoing footsteps mingled with the strains of birdsong.

Stepping across the cobblestone street that bordered Greyfriars Kirkyard, DI McKenzie made his way towards the warm glow of the Greyfriars Bobby pub. The familiar scent of malt and hops greeted him as he pushed open the heavy wooden door, the inner warmth in stark contrast to the crisp spring air accompanying him over the threshold.

Gordon Caldwell was polishing glasses behind the bar, his movements rhythmic and practiced. The low hum of conversation filled the space as couples and groups conversed over food and a pint. When the barman spotted McKenzie, he stopped polishing. The corners of his mouth lifted in a reserved smile; its bearer, wary. "Grant," he nodded the terse one-word greeting.

"Afternoon, Gordon," McKenzie approached the bar. "Busy, I see?"

"It's been like this all day. Can I get you anything?"

"Aye, I'll have coke." The DI reached into his trouser pocket for some change.

"So, what can I do for you this time?" Caldwell asked as he placed the drink in front of the detective. "I haven't been up to anything, if that's why you're here?"

Mckenzie held up his hand. "I'm not here to question you." The DI regretted the tension emanating from his friend. He leaned against the bar, the wood cool and solid beneath his hands. "I thought you should know, if you haven't heard already, we caught him... the attacker."

Caldwell nodded. "I heard about it last night. I saw it on the television. It was pretty dramatic. Best TV I've seen in ages..." He grimaced. "I'm sorry. I probably shouldn't joke about it. Was the wee lassie okay?"

"Aye, she will be."

"I'm glad. I think you catching the villain may be the reason people have returned to the bar. We went through a lean period the last few weeks. Folks too scared to come down here for fear of The Gimbal Killer."

"I'm glad they've made their way back." McKenzie sipped the cola, his tone one of sombre triumph. "The knife we took from our suspect was the murder weapon. And fibres matched samples taken from the sexual assault victims. We definitely have our man."

Gordon absorbed the information, his initial stoicism giving way to relief that rippled through him, easing the lines on his face. "That's good to hear, Grant. I'm pleased for you and the folks around here."

McKenzie pressed his lips together before continuing, "I thought you should know, given everything."

"Aye, thanks for telling me. I appreciate it," Gordon said, his voice regaining some of its old warmth. "Being on the suspect list was not the best experience."

"I imagine it wasn't..." McKenzie sighed. "I'm hoping we can put the past few months behind us. Start afresh?"

Gordon extended his hand over the counter. "Aye, water under the bridge."

THE AROMA of freshly brewed coffee permeated the briefing room at MIT in the Leith police station. McKenzie cradled a steaming mug between his hands, heat seeping through his palms as he leaned back in his chair. The team had gathered around the long table, with Rob Sinclair at the head.

"All right," the DCI's voice cut through the murmur of

post-operational chatter, commanding immediate attention. Eyes, sharp and approving, swept over his officers. "Take a moment, all of you. That was impressive work you did out there."

Grant caught the look of pride that flickered across Susan Robertson's usually stoic face, while Helen McAllister stopped twirling her pen, a habit she had when deep in thought. Graham Dalgliesh allowed himself a rare grin at the DCI, as he acknowledged their achievement.

"Thanks to your hard work," Sinclair continued, "we'll be seeing Tim Shaw in court sooner rather than later. Forensics are in no doubt he's our man for both the murders and sexual assaults."

McKenzie nodded, setting his coffee down. "His home was right slap-bang in the centre of the area Tam Fleming's geo-profiling pointed to. It's a shame he never knew just how well he had done at pinpointing the killer's lair."

"He was spot on," Sinclair agreed, his mouth pressed into a grim line.

"In fact, each of the victims contributed to finding the killer in their own way." McKenzie's gaze lingered on the case files piled in front of the DCI. "Their legacy helped stop Shaw from hurting anyone else."

"Here's to them," DS Robertson murmured, raising her coffee cup in a silent toast to the victims whose work had helped the team ensure justice.

"To them," DCI Sinclair echoed.

They raised their mugs in a synchronised salute to the murdered influencers.

~

THAT AFTERNOON, the DI was busy typing up final reports when Dalgleish plopped that day's newspapers in front of him. "MIT Heroes Apprehend The Gimbal Killer" and "Edinburgh Breathes Easier as Police Snag Killer."

"Wow, positive headlines for us for once, eh?" Grant perused the articles. "I wouldn't have believed it if I hadn't seen it for myself."

"Aye, we should make the most of it; cut them out and frame them." Graham grinned. "We're the topic of the day."

"Only until the next crisis hits the front page," McKenzie replied, fingers returning to his keyboard. "Fame is as fleeting as our Scottish sunshine."

"Still," the DC continued, leaning against the edge of McKenzie's desk and nodding towards the screen, "it's not every day you see your face on telly and don't have to change your name and flee the country."

The DI cracked a smile, finally looking at his colleague. "I'll remember to enjoy my fifteen minutes before I'm back to being an anonymous cog in the machine."

"Anonymous? With that brooding brow and the way you wear your existential angst like a badge? Not likely," the DC chuckled, snatching a newspaper from the pile and pretending to scrutinise McKenzie's photograph. "You're the poster boy for Scottish detective work; they'll be using your scowl to scare the recruits into line."

"Jings! I'd rather they use it to scare off criminals," Grant laughed, the banter giving him a much-needed, albeit brief, break from writing. He returned to his report, keystrokes resuming their steady tempo.

"Anyway," Dalgleish added, pushing away from the desk, "We've earned the good press. I'm going to milk it, so I am."

"You do that, Mate." McKenzie grinned. "But, if you'll

excuse me, I have to immortalise our heroic efforts in this report before Sinclair takes my cloak and superpowers."

"Aye, I'll leave you to it." Dalgliesh gave a mock salute as he left. "Carry on, sir. Immortalise away."

Pulling a face, the DI turned his attention back to his screen.

22

PEACE RETURNS

The clinking of crockery and the gentle scrape of cutlery against plates filled the warm kitchen at their home in The Grange. The DI smiled, surrounded by the comforting chaos of family. Rays of morning sunlight streamed through the window, casting a soft glow on his wife Jane's hair as she leaned over to wipe a smudge of jam from Martha's cheek. Davey and Craig fought over the last piece of toast.

"All right, you two," Grant leaned over, chuckling at the serious expressions on the faces of his two boys. "Share it... Go halves, remember?"

With a reluctant nod, Davey picked up a knife and tried sawing the toast down the middle, concentrating hard as he performed the task; tongue lolling at the side of his mouth.

"Your half is bigger than mine," Craig accused. "I want that one."

Their dad intervened, cutting the halves into quarters and divvying them up to his lads' satisfaction. It was small beans compared to policing, the minor tussles of family life. It was good to bask in the normalcy of a Saturday morning.

Jane, clearing the dishes away, quipped, "You know what this day is missing? A picnic in Princes Street Gardens. Fresh air, sandwiches, and a game of tag to give the little munchkins some running."

It was a light-hearted jest intended to draw a poke or a playful groan from her husband. But Davey's face lit up at the prospect of an adventure in the park, while little Craig's eyes sparkled with excitement at the thought of more food. Martha, too young to fully grasp the idea, simply mirrored her brothers' enthusiasm with a toothy grin and a clap of her hands.

Grant pulled a face at his wife. "Did you have to?" Her teasing was not lost on him. Looking at the children, he said, "How about we aim for somewhere with... towers and tales of old? Perhaps a fortress perched high above the city? Where dragons and pirates gang a creeping..."

His words, delivered in story mode with a rich Scottish accent, provided a gentle redirection, steering thoughts away from memories he was not ready to revisit. An after-noon of discovery and adventure at Edinburgh Castle held more appeal. There, the children could run around having imaginary battles while learning about Scottish ancestors.

"Great." Jane grinned. "I'll pack sandwiches."

The regal edifice stood atop the old volcano, keeping guard over the city, its strategic position having shaped centuries of Scottish history. Sweeping views, once used for defence, now offered panoramas that stole their breath, extending out toward the Firth of Forth and the hills beyond.

"Look at that cannon!" Davey dashed ahead toward Mons Meg, one of the finest medieval cannons ever made; a testament to the power struggles of bygone eras. Craig followed in his brother's wake, though more cautious, afraid the thing might go off.

"Don't go too far, lads," Grant called after them, unable to keep up.

Martha clung to her father's hand, her small frame dwarfed by the vastness of the castle courtyard. Her eyes were wide with wonder, each cobblestone and turret offering a new marvel. Together, they wandered through the Stone of Destiny's chamber, the fabled granite which had seen Scottish kings crowned as the DI wove tales of sovereignty and legend.

"Is this where the king lives?" Martha asked.

"Kings and queens once lived here," McKenzie replied, scooping her up to better see the Honours of Scotland, the crown jewels that rested securely behind glass, their splendour undiminished by time.

They roamed through the Great Hall, its hammer-beam roof impressive in both scale and craftsmanship. The DI recounted tales of grand banquets and royal gatherings, painting a picture of merriment that contrasted with the spectres of his recent work.

"Imagine the feasts they had here," Jane whispered to the children, her words conjuring images of tables laden with exotic fare and the air filled with music and laughter.

As they exited the hall, stepping back into the light of day, the DI felt gratitude for the respite the ancient fortress provided. Here, surrounded by his family amidst the shadows of history, the horror of the last few weeks dissipated for a while.

≈

≈

THE COBBLESTONES of the old street echoed under the DI's feet, a sombre rhythm matching his mood. He wasn't sure how this meeting would go, and whether he would find the delicate words needed. He paused before the imposing Georgian townhouse, whose facade spoke of Edinburgh's historic past. Checking his watch, he lifted the brass knocker and rapped twice.

For a moment, he thought no-one was home but, as he turned away, the door swung open, revealing Carol Fraser on the doorstep, looking sleepy in pyjamas and dressing gown; hair mussed as though she had woken only moments before. Her eyes, usually alive with curiosity, were dull and shadowed by her recent ordeal.

"May I come in?" Grant's voice carried a warmth he hoped would ease the tension he saw in her at his arrival.

"Of course," she replied, stepping aside. Her gaze flitted along the street as she shut the door behind him, a vigilance likely entrenched since her attack.

As he entered the hall, he noted the pristine condition of her home. She had rendered it spotless and gleaming. "Are you all right?" he asked, the concern in his voice genuine.

"Getting there," she answered, tightening the belt on her towelling dressing gown, a subtle sign of discomfort. "Tea is brewing. I'm expecting my mum shortly. Would you like a cup?"

"I would love a cup, yes, though I won't keep you long." He followed her into the kitchen where the bergamot scent of Earl Grey hung in the air. The DI sat at the marble island.

"Your attacker is behind bars where he belongs," he began. "I wanted to make sure you are getting the support you need, and we'll need a final statement from you."

"I'm lucky you guys arrived when you did," she said, eyes wistful. "At one point, I thought I was a goner. I cursed myself for being fooled into meeting the killer. He was Sally-One, pretending to be a woman afraid of someone she lived with."

McKenzie leaned forward, resting his forearms on the cool countertop. "We arrived because we saw the note you left for your mum. You know, if you continue in your line of work, you must be extremely cautious about meeting people, no matter how important you think their information might be. We are equipped to deal with surprises. We have tasers, pepper spray, handcuffs, and backup. You have none of those things. Dealing with criminals can be dangerous work."

She nodded. "I know. This... It was a wake-up call."

"Make sure your followers are cautious, too. The people they poke don't play by our rules. They won't hesitate to..." He trailed off. He wasn't here to teach her to suck eggs.

"We'll be more careful, I promise." Carol assured him. "I never intended to become a part of the story. I'll make sure my followers know the dangers."

"Thank you." He nodded. "Your safety is paramount."

The influencer spent the following twenty minutes giving and signing her statement before the DI got up to leave.

"Carol," he said, voice low but clear in the quiet that had settled in the home. "One more thing before I go."

She tilted her head. "Yes?"

"Should you ever find yourself knee-deep in something that feels dangerous, don't think twice about reaching out to us at MIT."

"Are you after intel?" she smiled, brow arching.

"You could be useful," Grant grinned at her. "Seriously though, if you ever think you are onto a killer, don't go chasing them yourself. Clue us in. We deal with that sort of risk every day. It's what we do."

"I will let you know." She opened the door for him. "It's reassuring, thank you."

"It's not just about reassurance." His eyes held hers, earnest and unyielding. "It's practical. We have resources. Networks. Experience with these sorts of predators. You've got a platform and a voice and can make waves, Sure. It's a powerful thing to have, but it can also paint a target on your back."

"Understood," she responded, her posture straightening at the gravity of his words. "I'll keep that in mind."

"Please do," he insisted, stepping out onto the street. "And don't hesitate. Any hour; any day. If it's urgent, we move fast."

"Any hour?" She teased, a flicker of her influencer charm shining through the solemn moment.

"If it's the middle of the night, dial nine-nine-nine." He grinned, turning away. "Take care, Carol."

THE CLATTER of metal on metal echoed as the cell door slammed shut, sealing Tim Shaw within the cold, grey walls of HMP Edinburgh. He paced the narrow space like a caged animal, his footsteps muffled by prison-issue slippers that served as his only comfort against the cold floor.

"Oi, Gimbal!" a voice jeered from a nearby cell, a mocking reference to his grim sobriquet in the press. "How's the accommodation?"

Shaw's jaw clenched, his dark eyes flicking towards the

source of the ridicule. He didn't grace the question with a response; instead, sinking onto the edge of his hard bunk bed, springs groaning under the weight.

"Come on, killer, ain't it cosy enough for ya?" another inmate taunted.

"Shut it." His growled response held an unmistakable menace. He lay down, staring at peeling paint on the wall as though he could burn holes through it, and into the inmate in the next cell, with sheer force of will.

"Bet you miss your fancy gadgets now, eh? No gimbals here, just good old locks and bars," a third voice called, laughing at his own words. Saughton Prison was a far cry from Shaw's meticulous home.

Meal times were no better. He eyed the slop they called dinner with disgust—the overcooked vegetables, the stodgy lump masquerading as potato, and the meagre meat portions.

"You have a problem with that?" a thickset man with the serving spoon asked, as he doled on a splash of gravy.

"It looks like you scraped it off the kitchen floor," Tim muttered, pushing the tray along with a sneer.

"Better get used to it, Gimbal. That's gourmet compared to what you'll get once they put you away for good." The kitchen assistant's voice faded away as Shaw seated himself at a table. The disdain he felt for his surroundings, the prisoners, and the barely edible food provided fuel to keep the defiance burning.

"Thinking about your big day, Shaw?" A guard's voice cut through his thoughts, a jibe dressed as small talk.

"Counting down the moments," he replied, voice smooth as the blade he was infamous for wielding. "I don't intend being here long."

The guard snorted in disbelief. "You really think you're walking out of here?"

"Watch me." Shaw's eyes didn't waver, crystalline blue and intense. "The prosecution's case is nothing but smoke."

"Keep telling yourself that." The disinterested guard walked away, leaving the psychopath alone.

THE END

AFTERWORD

Watch out for Book 2 in the DI McKenzie Series, coming soon...

Mailing list: You can join my emailing list here : AnnamarieMorgan.com

Facebook page: AnnamarieMorganAuthor

Book 1: Murder on Arthur's Seat

When DI Grant McKenzie's world is thrown into chaos by the sudden disappearance of his twenty-one-year-old nephew, he is determined to uncover the truth no matter the cost.

As he and his team are plunged into a dark and sinister web of organised crime, McKenzie must face a wealthy and elusive kingpin who believes himself untouchable. With the fate of his nephew hanging in the balance, McKenzie and his team will stop at nothing to bring the criminal mastermind to justice.

You might also like to read the author's other books.

The DI Giles Series:

Book 1: Death Master:

After months of mental and physical therapy, Yvonne Giles, an Oxford DI, is back at work and that's just how she likes it. So when she's asked to hunt the serial killer responsible for taking apart young women, the DI jumps at the chance but hides the fact she is suffering debilitating flashbacks. She is told to work with Tasha Phillips, an in-her-face, criminal psychologist. The DI is not enamoured with the idea. Tasha has a lot to prove. Yvonne has a lot to get over. A tentative link with a 20 year-old cold case brings them closer to the truth but events then take a horrifyingly personal turn.

Book 2: You Will Die

After apprehending an Oxford Serial Killer, and almost losing her life in the process, DI Yvonne Giles has left England for a quieter life in rural Wales.Her peace is shattered when she is asked to hunt a priest-killing psychopath, who taunts the police with messages inscribed on the corpses.Yvonne requests the help of Dr. Tasha Phillips, a psychologist and friend, to aid in the hunt. But the killer is one step ahead and the ultimatum, he sets them, could leave everyone devastated.

Book 3: Total Wipeout

A whole family is wiped out with a shotgun. At first glance, it's an open-and-shut case. The dad did it, then killed himself. The deaths follow at least two similar family wipeouts – attributed to the financial crash.

So why doesn't that sit right with Detective Inspector Yvonne Giles? And why has a rape occurred in the area, in the weeks preceding each family's demise? Her seniors do not believe there are questions to answer. DI Giles must therefore risk everything, in a high-stakes investigation ofa mysterious masonic ring and players in high finance.

Can she find the answers, before the next innocent family is wiped out?

Book 4: Deep Cut

In a tiny hamlet in North Wales, a female recruit is murdered whilst on Christmas home leave. Detective Inspector Yvonne Giles is asked to cut short her own leave, to investigate. Why was the young soldier killed? And is her death related to several alleged suicides at her army base? DI Giles this it is, and that someone powerful has a dark secret they will do anything to hide.

Book 5: The Pusher

Young men are turning up dead on the banks of the River Severn. Some of them have been missing for days or even weeks. The only thing the police can be sure of, is that the men have drowned. Rumours abound that a mythical serial killer has turned his attention from the Manchester canal to the waterways of Mid-Wales. And now one of CID's own is missing. A brand new recruit with everything to live for. DI Giles must find him before it's too late.

Book 6: Gone

Children are going missing. They are not heard from again until sinister requests for cryptocurrency go viral. The public must pay or the children die. For lead detective Yvonne Giles, the case is complicated enough. And then the unthinkable happens...

Book 7: Bone Dancer

A serial killer is murdering women, threading their

bones back together, and leaving them for police to find. Detective Inspector Yvonne Giles must find him before more innocent victims die. Problem is, the killer wants her and will do anything he can to get her. Unaware that she, herself, is is a target, DI Giles risks everything to catch him.

Book 8: Blood Lost

A young man comes home to find his whole family missing. Half-eaten breakfasts and blood spatter on the lounge wall are the only clues to what happened...

Book 9: Angel of Death

The peace of the Mid-Wales countryside is shattered, when a female eco-warrior is found crucified in a public wood. At first, it would appear a simple case of finding which of the woman's enemies had had her killed. But DI Yvonne Giles has no idea how bad things are going to get. As the body count rises, she will need all of her instincts, and the skills of those closest to her, to stop the murderous rampage of the Angel of Death.

Book 10: Death in the Air

Several fatal air collisions have occurred within a few months in rural Wales. According to the local Air Accidents Investigation Branch (AAIB) inspector, it's a coincidence. Clusters happen. Except, this cluster is different. DI Yvonne Giles suspects it when she hears some of the witness statements but, when an AAIB inspector is found dead under a bridge, she knows it.

Something is way off. Yvonne is determined to get to the bottom of the mystery, but exactly how far down the treacherous rabbit hole is she prepared to go?

Book 11: Death in the Mist

The morning after a viscous sea-mist covers the seaside town of Aberystwyth, a young student lies brutalised within one hundred yards of the castle ruins.

DI Yvonne Giles' reputation precedes her. Having successfully captured more serial killers than some detectives have caught colds, she is seconded to head the murder investigation team, and hunt down the young woman's killer.

What she doesn't know, is this is only the beginning...

Book 12: Death under Hypnosis

When the secretive and mysterious Sheila Winters approaches Yvonne Giles and tells her that she murdered someone thirty years before, she has the DI's immediate attention.

Things get even more strange when Sheila states:

She doesn't know who.

She doesn't know where.

She doesn't know why.

Book 13: Fatal Turn

A seasoned hiker goes missing from the Dolfor Moors after recording a social media video describing a narrow cave he intends to explore. A tragic accident? Nothing to see here, until a team of cavers disappear on a coastal potholing expedition, setting off a string of events that has DI Giles tearing her hair out. What, or who is the thread that ties this series of disappearances together?

A serial killer, thriller murder-mystery set in Wales.

Book 14: The Edinburgh Murders

A newly-retired detective from the Met is murdered in a

murky alley in Edinburgh, a sinister calling card left with the body.

The dead man had been a close friend of psychologist Tasha Phillips, giving her her first gig with the Met decades before.

Tasha begs DI Yvonne Giles to aid the Scottish police in solving the case.

In unfamiliar territory, and with a ruthless killer haunting the streets, the DI plunges herself into one of the darkest, most terrifying cases of her career. Who exactly is The Poet?

Book 15: A Picture of Murder

Men are being thrown to their deaths in rural Wales.

At first glance, the murders appear unconnected until DI Giles uncovers potential links with a cold case from the turn of the Millennium.

Someone is eliminating the witnesses to a double murder.

DI Giles and her team must find the perpetrator before all the witnesses are dead.

Book 16: The Wilderness Murders

People are disappearing from remote locations.

Abandoned cars, neatly piled belongings, and bizarre last photographs, are the only clues for what happened to them.

Did they run away? Or, as DI Giles suspects, have they fallen prey to a serial killer who is taunting police with the heinous pieces of a puzzle they must solve if they are to stop the wilderness murderer.

Book 17: The Bunker Murders

A murder victim found in a shallow grave has DI Yvonne Giles and her team on the hunt for both the killer and a motive for the well-loved man's demise.

Yvonne cannot help feeling the killing is linked to a string of female disappearances stretching back nearly two decades.

Someone has all the answers, and the DI will stop at nothing to find them and get to the bottom of this perplexing mystery.

Book 18: The Garthmyl Murders

A missing brother and friends with dark secrets have DI Giles turning circles after a body is found face-down in the pond of a local landmark.

Stymied by a wall of silence and superstition, Yvonne and her team must dig deeper than ever if they are to crack this impossible case.

Who, or what, is responsible for the Garthmyl murders?

Book 19: The Signature

When a young woman is found dead inside a rubbish dumpster after a night out, police chiefs are quick to label it a tragic accident. But as more bodies surface, Detective Inspector Yvonne Giles is convinced a cold-blooded murderer is on the loose. She believes the perpetrator is devious and elusive, disabling CCTV cameras in the area, and leaving them with little to go on. With time running out, Giles and her team must race against the clock to catch the killer or killers before they strike again.

Book 20: The Incendiary Murders

When the Powys mansion belonging to an ageing rock star is rocked by a deadly explosion, Detective Inspector

Yvonne Giles finds herself tasked with a case of murder, suspicion, and secrets. As shockwaves ripple through the community, Giles must pierce the impenetrable facades of the characters surrounding the case, racing the clock to find the culprit and prevent further bombings. With an investigation full of twists and turns, DI Yvonne Giles must unravel the truth before it's too late.

Book 21 - The Park Murders

When two people are left dead and four others are seriously ill in hospital after a visit to a local nature park in rural Wales, DI Giles and her team find themselves in a race against time to stop a killer or killers hell-bent on terrorising the community. As the investigation deepens, the team must draw on all of their skill and experience to hunt down the elusive Powys poisoner before more lives are lost.

Remember to watch out for Book 22 in the DI Giles Series, coming soon...

Printed in Great Britain
by Amazon

This book is for Harold and Adrienne Streeter

Little my soul,
You and I are the same...
MARK VAN DOREN,
"LITTLE MY SOUL"

CONTENTS

Acknowledgments ~ xi

Introduction ~ xiii

1. Listen to Your Deepest Self ~ 1

2. Begin Your Day With Prayer ~ 2

3. End Your Day With Prayer ~ 3

4. Do Work You Enjoy ~ 5

5. Listen to Music ~ 6

6. Learn a Poem by Heart ~ 7

7. Laugh Until You Cry ~ 9

8. Look at Some Old Photographs ~ 10

9. Grow Older With Grace ~ 12

10. Write a Poem ~ 13

11. Practice Meditation ~ 15

12. Play a Musical Instrument ~ 16

13. Enjoy Your Sexuality ~ 18

14. Read a Good Book ~ 19

15. Spend Time in Quiet Solitude ~ 21

16. Keep a Journal ~ 22

17. Cultivate Your Marriage ~ 23

18. Trust Your Higher Power ~ 25

19. Sing a Song ~ 26

20. Visit a Museum ~ 27

21. Give Away Something You Cherish ~ 29

22. Belong to a Believing Community ~ 30

23. Breathe In and Out ~ 32

24. Take a Day Off ~ 33

25. Write a Letter to an Old Friend ~ 34

26. Read a Book You Wouldn't Ordinarily Read ~ 36

27. Watch Classic Comedy, and Laugh Again ~ 37

28. Give Up Bitterness ~ 38

29. Visit Someone Who Is Lonely ~ 40

30. Be a Kind and Considerate Driver ~ 41

31. Look at Your Hands for Five Minutes ~ 43

32. Think About Your Children ~ 44

33. Be Open to Possible Miracles ~ 45

34. Prepare a Wonderful Dinner at Home ~ 47

35. Get a Physical Checkup ~ 48

36. Become a Prayerful Person ~ 49

37. Be Generous to the Point of Extravagance ~ 51

38. Take a Walk ~ 52

39. Accept Praise ~ 54

40. Do the Right Thing ~ 55

41. Listen to Your Heartbeat ~ 56

42. Visit a Zoo ~ 58

43. Participate in Formal Worship ~ 59

44. Light a Candle ~ 60

45. Get Socially Involved ~ 62

46. Forgive Someone Who Did You Some Wrong ~ 63